"She-Devil..."

"Is that what you think of me?" Lyric asked.

Trevor set his hat more firmly on his head. "Let's just say that I don't think much of a woman who kisses one man while engaged to another."

"Lyle needed me—especially after the accident."

"The car wreck wasn't all that serious," Trevor said with undisguised bitterness. "It didn't maim him or call for a life-or-death operation, did it?"

Lyric hesitated. "No," she said. "It didn't."

"Would you have broken the engagement and come to me...if I'd asked?"

Lyric thought of endless nights at the hospital, Lyle thinking that he was going to be all right, not realizing he was slipping further and further away...

Studying the strong, healthy man beside her, she sighed. "No. I couldn't have come then."

Trevor's face hardened. "Then why the hell did you come now?"

Dear Reader,

It's hard to believe that it's *that* time of year again—and what better way to escape the holiday hysteria than with a good book…or six! Our selections begin with Allison Leigh's *The Truth About the Tycoon,* as a man bent on revenge finds his plans have hit a snag—in the form of the beautiful sister of the man he's out to get.

THE PARKS EMPIRE concludes its six-book run with *The Homecoming* by Gina Wilkins, in which Walter Parks's daughter tries to free her mother from the clutches of her unscrupulous father. Too bad the handsome detective working for her dad is hot on her trail! *The M.D.'s Surprise Family* by Marie Ferrarella is another in her popular miniseries THE BACHELORS OF BLAIR MEMORIAL. This time, a lonely woman looking for a doctor to save her little brother finds both a healer of bodies and of hearts in the handsome neurosurgeon who comes highly recommended. In *A Kiss in the Moonlight,* another in Laurie Paige's SEVEN DEVILS miniseries, a woman can't resist her attraction to the man she let get away—because guilt was pulling her in another direction. But now he's back in her sights—soon to be in her clutches? In Karen Rose Smith's *Which Child Is Mine?* a woman is torn between the child she gave birth to and the one she's been raising. And the only way out seems to be to marry the man who fathered her "daughter." Last, a man decides to reclaim everything he's always wanted, in the form of his biological daughters, and their mother, in Sharon De Vita's *Rightfully His.*

Here's hoping every one of your holiday wishes comes true, and we look forward to celebrating the New Year with you.

All the best,

Gail Chasan
Senior Editor

Please address questions and book requests to:
Silhouette Reader Service
U.S.: 3010 Walden Ave., P.O. Box 1325, Buffalo, NY 14269
Canadian: P.O. Box 609, Fort Erie, Ont. L2A 5X3

G.

A Kiss in the Moonlight

LAURIE PAIGE

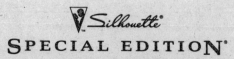

Silhouette

SPECIAL EDITION

Published by Silhouette Books

America's Publisher of Contemporary Romance

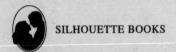 **SILHOUETTE BOOKS**

ISBN 0-373-24654-4

A KISS IN THE MOONLIGHT

Visit Silhouette Books at www.eHarlequin.com

Printed in U.S.A.

Books by Laurie Paige

LAURIE PAIGE

Laurie has been a NASA engineer, a past president of the Romance Writers of America, a mother and a grandmother. She was twice a Romance Writers of America RITA® finalist for Best Traditional Romance and has won awards from *Romantic Times* for Best Silhouette Special Edition and Best Silhouette in addition to appearing on the *USA TODAY* bestseller list. Recently resettled in Northern California, Laurie is looking forward to whatever experiences her next novel will send her on.

DALTON FAMILY TREE

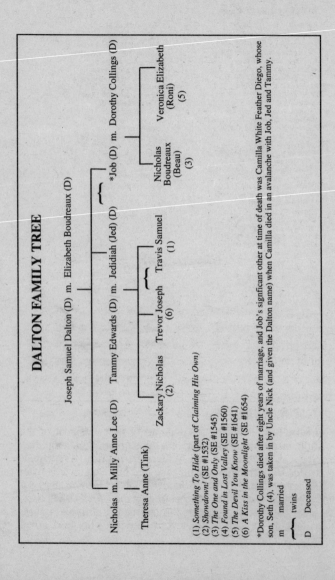

Joseph Samuel Dalton (D) m. Elizabeth Boudreaux (D)

Tammy Edwards (D) m. Jedidiah (Jed) (D)

*Job (D) m. Dorothy Collings (D)

Nicholas m. Milly Anne Lee (D)

Theresa Anne (Tink)

Zackary Nicholas
(2)

Trevor Joseph
(6)

Travis Samuel
(1)

Nicholas Boudreaux
(Beau)
(3)

Veronica Elizabeth
(Roni)
(5)

(1) *Something To Hide* (part of *Claiming His Own*)
(2) *Showdown!* (SE #1532)
(3) *The One and Only* (SE #1545)
(4) *Found in Lost Valley* (SE #1560)
(5) *The Devil You Know* (SE #1641)
(6) *A Kiss in the Moonlight* (SE #1654)

*Dorothy Collings died after eight years of marriage, and Job's significant other at time of death was Camilla White Feather Diego, whose son, Seth (4), was taken in by Uncle Nick (and given the Dalton name) when Camilla died in an avalanche with Job, Jed and Tammy.

m   married

{   twins

D   Deceased

Chapter One

Lyric Gibson felt the headache as a throb centered behind her eyes. She tried to consciously relax the tension that tightened the muscles of her forehead and those across her shoulders. That worked as long as she concentrated, but she was looking for road signs, and her attention was on that task.

"Have we passed it, do you think?" her great-aunt, Fay Gibson, asked in slightly querulous tones.

Lyric flinched as guilt joined the other emotions that swirled through her innermost self. She should have stopped in Boise for the night. Her aunt was sixty-eight years old and, although usually cheerful and persevering, much too tired from the long hours they'd spent on the road.

But it had been early afternoon—not quite four— so there'd been hours of July daylight left when they'd driven through the city. The mountain town of Lost Valley was only an hour north of there, according to her information, so she'd pushed on. They'd found the town without a problem.

The Seven Devils Ranch, their hoped-for destination, was supposed to be less than an hour west of Lost Valley, so they should have arrived by six at the latest.

It was now half past eight.

She had no idea if they were any closer to their destination now than they'd been an hour ago. Glancing at the western sky, she fought worry and the headache that accompanied it. She was no longer sure where they were. The back roads of Idaho all looked the same, and she'd obviously taken a couple of wrong turns. Or three or four.

Maybe this whole trip was a mistake. She'd been stunned when her great-aunt had delivered the invitation that had included her. Then she'd been elated. Now she was simply unsure.

"It'll be dark soon," Aunt Fay said, then gave an impatient *tsk*. "I'm sorry, Lyric. I shouldn't have said that. I know you're concerned about me, but this wouldn't be the first time I've been lost and slept in a car."

Lyric managed a confident laugh. "We'll find it. We're bound to be close. We passed a sign that said He-Devil Mountain was thataway." She pointed toward the west. "The ranch is supposed to be within sight of the peak. We're just taking the scenic route."

A shiver ran over every nerve in her body as she recalled a dark-haired, blue-eyed, tall, handsome cowboy who'd once told her about his family's ranch and its splendid view, its crystal streams and lakes, the majestic sweep of the land.

She'd longed to explore the mountains and valleys with him, but fate had intervened, temporarily at any rate.

Trevor had listened to her rushed, disjointed explanation of why she'd had to leave, first in disbelief then with growing anger. With his jaw set as hard as stone, he'd nodded as if he understood, but then he'd left. Without a word. Without a backward glance.

That had been almost a year ago.

During the endless fall and winter, through storms that brought floods to much of the southwest, she'd waited, sure he would write. But he hadn't contacted her, not even when she'd sent a note that explained more fully. She'd given up hope. Then out of the blue came an invitation to visit the ranch. That had to mean something.

She put the shaky elation and haunting doubts aside to concentrate on finding the right road. She didn't want to make another wrong turn.

"I see a trail of dust," she said, peering through her driving glasses at this welcome indication of another vehicle. It was on a side road off to the right of the county road they traveled, which was also a gravel surface. The other driver had probably seen her dust, too.

The earlier concern eased a bit. "We can stop the driver and get directions."

"He's coming awfully fast. Be careful. He may be a rustler or something."

Lyric cast her aunt a partly amused, partly exasperated glance at this bit of advice.

Rustlers? Ask her if she cared.

She slowed in anticipation of flagging the oncoming vehicle at the intersection of the two roads. "At present, I'd face down the devil himself if he would help get us to our destination."

Her aunt laughed at the quip. The older woman was like a grandmother to Lyric and her two younger brothers. Aunt Fay had never married, but she'd taken in her nephew, Lyric's father, years ago when his parents had died in a traffic accident. She'd always treated the family as if they were her children.

"Oh!" the spinster gasped.

Lyric swung the steering wheel hard to the right as a truck tore out of the gravel side road at breakneck speed and nearly hit them. She felt the compact station wagon graze a large rock as they careened into a shallow ditch at the side of the road.

The back tires slid sideways. She turned into the skid and took her foot off the brake. The rear skittered back and forth on the loose gravel. As the tires regained traction and she had the car under control once more, a pile of stones encased in a section of fence to form a corner post loomed before them.

''Oh, no,'' she said.

They hit the stones with a resounding thud.

Air bags blossomed on each side of the front seat. Lyric spared a worry for her relative as the bag hit her face, smothering her for a few seconds and pressing her glasses painfully onto her nose.

Dizzy and frightened, Lyric remembered to turn the engine off, then she thrashed her way free of the collapsing air bag and turned to her aunt. After pushing the plastic aside, Lyric searched the older woman's face for damage.

''Aunt Fay?'' she said.

The other woman didn't answer, didn't move.

''Hey, are you okay in there?'' a male voice asked.

''My aunt,'' Lyric said. ''I think she's hurt.'' She snapped open the seat belt and reached for her aunt's wrist to check her pulse.

''Don't move her,'' the man ordered.

He went around the station wagon and opened the door. With a competence that was reassuring, he checked the unconscious woman after removing her glasses, which by some miracle weren't broken, and sticking them in his pocket.

Lyric watched his hands run gently over Aunt Fay's head, down her neck, where he paused to check her pulse, then continue over her shoulders and along her arms. His fingers were long and slender, the skin evenly tanned to where the white shirtsleeves were rolled up on his forearms. A hat hid most of his face. He bent farther into the car and examined her aunt's knees and legs.

Lyric looked, too, and saw red marks indicating the bruises that would be forming soon.

He raised his head. "Ms. Gibson?" he said. "Can you hear me? Can you open your eyes?"

Lyric's heart stopped, then pounded with a fierce, staccato beat. She gasped like a heroine in a melodrama as she studied the man in disbelief.

"Trevor?"

He faced her then, his eyes, which she knew to be as blue as the summer sky, appearing dark as midnight in the fading glow of the sunset. "Yeah, it's me."

They stared at each other in silence, a thousand questions and memories wrapping around their frozen forms. One thing for sure—there was no welcome in his gaze.

Aunt Fay opened her eyes and focused on one, then the other of them. "Where are my glasses?"

"Here," Trevor said. He slipped the thin gold frames gently onto the older woman's face.

"Are you all right?" Lyric asked, searching her beloved relative's face for signs of pain.

"I've felt better," her aunt said, then gave the man a smile. "Hello, Trevor. How are you?"

"I'm okay...other than feeling like a heel. There isn't usually much traffic out this way."

"I'm sure," her aunt agreed with dry humor.

"Let me check the damage to your car, then we'll see if it'll run. It's only a couple of miles to the ranch." He paused and looked at Lyric. "How did you get on this back road, anyway?"

"A seriously wrong turn, I think."

He nodded, his face grim but otherwise without expression. After getting a flashlight from his truck, he looked over the front end of the station wagon. "A badly dinged bumper and a slightly crumpled nose, but otherwise it looks okay. The radiator seems intact. I don't see any fluid leaking out. Crank it up and let's see if she'll run."

Lyric turned on the key. The engine purred to life at once. Trevor returned to the front of the vehicle. He nodded in her direction, indicating everything looked fine.

"Back up," he said, coming to her window. "Keep the wheels straight."

She cautiously backed onto the road. Trevor gave the car a push when one tire slipped on the gravel and dirt in the shallow ditch.

"Okay," he called when she was clear. "Follow me."

After he turned his truck around, she fell into place behind him, far enough back that his dust didn't choke them. In less than five minutes they pulled up before a horse rail in front of a sprawling ranch house, its center portion made of massive logs, the wings on either side more modern structures of stone and wood.

Trevor honked his horn, then climbed out of the

truck and came to the passenger side of the station wagon. "Watch your step now," he said to Aunt Fay. "Careful. Lean on me while we see if your legs are okay. You have pain anywhere?"

"I'm not sure," the older woman said. "I seem to be numb at the moment."

With the gentlest of care, he escorted her aunt toward the house. The door opened and an older man peered out. His hair gleamed silver in the light from the room behind him. He was as tall as Trevor and had the same lean, rangy frame.

A total stranger would have known they were kin at a glance. The man had to be Trevor's uncle Nick.

"What happened?" Mr. Dalton asked, realizing something was wrong.

"Accident," Trevor said. He quickly explained about taking the old logging road and cutting the station wagon off at the county road, causing her to run into the ditch.

The older man came out on the porch, then stepped down on a giant flat granite boulder that served as the step to the front porch that ran all the way across the log portion of the house.

"My God," he said. "Fay, is that you?"

"Yes, Nick," her aunt replied with a smile in his direction. She clasped Trevor's arm and walked with a decided limp toward the porch.

"I'd given up on you for today." The Dalton uncle, wearing only socks, rushed to her other side and wrapped a supporting arm around her waist. "Call

Beau,'' he ordered his nephew. ''He's a doctor,'' he said to Lyric's aunt.

''Let's get the women in the house first,'' Trevor suggested with a hint of impatience.

Lyric followed behind the three, rather like a stray pup who hoped the others would take her in. She was beginning to feel very apprehensive about being here. Trevor didn't seem thrilled to see her.

In the house, after Aunt Fay was seated in an easy chair and checked over again, Lyric stood inside the door and wondered what to do.

Finally the older man noticed her. ''Are you all right?''

Lyric nodded. She had to clear her throat in order to talk. ''Yes. I think so,'' she amended, suddenly aware of pain in her knees, as if her body had come back to life at that instant and now reminded her of aches she hadn't known she had.

''Nicholas?''

The Dalton patriarch turned back to her aunt and took her hand. ''Now don't you worry about a thing. We'll have you right as rain in no time. Trevor, have you called Beau yet?'' he questioned with a stern glance at his nephew.

Lyric was aware of Trevor's gaze on her, of the tight set of his mouth, of the unwelcoming stance in his strong, lithe body. She felt terribly confused and disoriented.

He turned away. ''I'm doing it now.'' He went into

the kitchen. In a minute she heard his voice explaining the situation to the nephew who was a doctor.

Lyric hadn't met any of the Dalton family except Trevor, but she knew them all. Her aunt Fay had been a cousin and best friend to Milly Dalton, who had been married to Trevor's uncle Nick. Milly had died in an automobile accident many years ago. Their daughter, Tink, had been taken from the scene of the accident and never found again.

At least, that was what was assumed. The three-year-old had disappeared. She could have wandered away and died in the wilderness, but the sheriff had concluded the child had been abducted for some reason, because the child's body had never been found.

A tremor rushed over Lyric at the thought. One time a stranger had tried to grab her while she was on her way home from school in Austin, Texas.

She'd screamed and kicked and bit the man as hard as she could, the way her father had taught her, and had gotten free. She'd been lucky. A schoolmate on the next block had been kidnapped later the same afternoon. A month went by before the body was found in a lonely section of woods. That summer Lyric's parents had moved to the ranch her father had inherited from his dad.

Another tremor ran down her body and lodged in her legs. Alarmed, she realized her knees were about to give way. "I'm sorry," she said, "but…"

The words were barely a whisper.

She tried again. "I'm sorry, but…"

"Catch her," a voice said from far away as the room became dark and mysterious.

Lyric blinked rapidly as strong arms closed around her. She knew these arms, this embrace.

Pressing her face into the clean expanse of the white shirt, she inhaled deeply and was filled with the scent of masculine aftershave, fresh-as-the-outdoors laundry and something more—a faint aroma that she recognized somewhere deep inside her. Yes, she knew this man.

She relaxed as he lifted her. She looped her arms around his shoulders and closed her eyes. Safe. She was safe. And home. Home at last.

"Here," Trevor said, putting Lyric on the leather sofa. "Lie still," he ordered when she started to sit up. He removed the glasses from her face, then winced at the redness on each side of her nose and running down under her eyes. The air bag had hit her hard, he realized. He laid the glasses on the end table.

A memory wafted into his mind—him removing her glasses, her laughing protests about not being able to see, his suggestion that she close her eyes, then the kisses...the hotter-than-molten-steel kisses, the fireworks that had gone off in his brain, stunning him with the force of the passion between them...and the feelings, the found-my-other-half joy of holding her....

"Get some ice," his uncle said. "Fay needs some on her face and knees."

"So does Lyric," Trevor said.

His throat closed after he said the name. Last fall he'd vowed never to say it again.

He silently mouthed all the expletives he could remember while going to the kitchen and grabbing several first-aid ice bags from the freezer. The ranch always had a good supply of such items on hand for the occasional kick from a recalcitrant horse or stubborn cow.

Along with dish towels and clothespins, he took the ice bags to the living room.

"When will Beau be here?" his uncle asked.

"He won't. He and the midwife have a difficult delivery going on. Since nothing is broken or bleeding and they're both coherent, he said to bring them to the clinic in the morning and he'd check them out."

"Mmm," Uncle Nick said in his disapproving tone.

Ignoring Lyric, who now sat upright and as prim as a spinster, Trevor ministered to her aunt, affixing two ice bags and dish towels to her knees with the clothespins and advising her to put the other on her face.

Finished, he went to Lyric. "Put this on your nose," he said, handing over the wrapped bag and noting the glasses were back in place. He couldn't help but steal a glance at her left hand and the bare ring finger. Forcing his gaze to the task at hand, he knelt and, as careful as a doctor performing brain surgery, rolled up her pants.

He winced when he saw the abraded skin of her knees and the blotches that indicated more extensive bruising than her aunt had suffered. As the driver, she'd had her seat closer to the dashboard so she could reach the brake pedal and accelerator. That meant she'd hit the dash harder.

At five feet, five inches, she'd felt small and delicate in his arms. But curvy. For months after he'd come back to the ranch, he would wake from a sound sleep, clutching the pillow to his chest, and know he'd been dreaming about her, about the way she'd felt cuddled against him.

However, he and Lyric had never slept together. She'd been engaged to another guy the whole time she'd been responding to his caresses.

Mentally cursing, he forced the memory into the battered tin box of the past. He was over it now, over her and the wild emotion he'd thought was love. A cheating woman wasn't on his list of most-wanted things.

Quickly, he secured the ice packs on her knees and moved away from the smoothness of her skin, the warmth of her body, the spicy scent of her powder and cologne.

"Have you two had dinner?" Uncle Nick asked.

"Yes," Lyric answered.

"No," her aunt said at the same time. The older woman continued, "Lyric was so anxious to get here that she didn't want to stop, so we had a salad at a fast-food place in Boise. That was hours ago. If I could bother you for some toast, that would be plenty for me.''

''I recall that you like chocolate cake with ice cream,'' Uncle Nick said, his eyes all soft and glowing.

Lyric's aunt removed the ice pack from her nose and grinned at the older man. ''You don't happen to have some of that, do you?''

''Well, now, I reckon we do.'' He rose from the matching chair next to the aunt's with a big smile. ''You ladies sit still. Trev and I will get it.''

Trevor refrained from rolling his eyes at his uncle's gallant manner. If the old man sparkled much more, they could wire him up to the light bulbs and save the cost of the electricity.

He followed the other man into the kitchen and helped prepare the treat. Glancing at the freshly made cake and the homemade ice cream, he frowned, recalling the way his uncle had insisted on preparing the dessert, even though the Fourth of July had been last week, which was when they usually made ice cream, and this was Tuesday, July the eighth. Since none of the orphaned Dalton cousins that Uncle Nick had taken in and raised as his own were expected at the ranch—they were all busy with new wives and jobs and the like—he'd wondered at the reason for the unusual activity.

Setting his jaw, he admitted he hadn't suspected a

thing, even though his uncle had made it plain he hadn't wanted Trevor to head over to a neighboring ranch for a visit that evening.

Glancing toward the living room, he said in a low voice, "You knew they were coming, didn't you?"

Uncle Nick nodded, busily spooning ice cream onto the saucers. "Fay and I have kept in touch for years, mostly cards at Christmas. She said she was restless and lonely this past winter, so I told her to come up for the wildflowers this spring, but she couldn't make it until her niece had time to drive her."

"You could have told *me*."

Eyes as blue as his own glanced his way. "I did. Last month, right after we got things straightened out between Roni and Adam. I distinctly recall mentioning it at Sunday dinner when everyone was here."

In May, Roni, one of the orphaned cousins and the only girl in the family, had married Adam. His younger sister, Honey, was married to Trevor's older brother, Zack.

Trevor sighed. The family connections were becoming complicated, with his two brothers and his three cousins all getting hitched during the prior fourteen months.

Five weddings.

He was the only bachelor left of the six kids whose four parents had been wiped out in a freak avalanche twenty-three years ago. His father and uncle had been twins, the same as he and Travis were. Uncle Nick, the oldest of the three Dalton brothers, and Aunt

Milly had taken all six children in and raised them as their own.

Glancing at the older man, who was acting as frisky as a new colt, Trevor experienced a clenching in the vicinity of his heart. Uncle Nick seemed okay now, but he'd had a heart attack last spring and a couple of weak spells since then.

Trevor heaved another sigh. If his uncle wanted to invite his deceased wife's cousin to visit, there was nothing he could do about it. Why Lyric had come with her aunt was the thing he didn't get.

Pasting a pleasant—he hoped—smile on his face, he carried two plates into the other room and gave one to Lyric while his uncle presented one to the aunt, then took the chair beside her and attentively asked about the trip and all that had been happening to her of late.

Trevor sat on the far end of the sofa from Lyric. Neither of them said a word for the next fifteen minutes.

"Trev, would you take the plates to the kitchen and bring out the coffee?" Uncle Nick turned to Fay. "I put on a pot of decaffeinated coffee. It should be ready. I find I can't sleep if I drink regular coffee at night."

"I have the same problem," she said.

Trevor met Lyric's gaze, and they exchanged spontaneous smiles as the older couple discussed aging and the changes it brought.

Lyric's eyes reminded him of a brown velvet dress

Aunt Milly had loved to wear. As a kid he'd once stroked the soft material and observed the way the light changed when the nap was smoothed down. Lyric's eyes were like that—changing from brown to gold as the light reflected off the golden flecks around the black pupil.

He wiped the smile off and looked away. He wanted nothing to do with her. No memories, no shared amusement over the old folks, nothing!

"I'll get the coffee," he said.

In the kitchen he sucked in a harsh breath and wondered how long this visit was going to last. Not that he wouldn't get through it just fine. After all, no one in his family knew he'd made a fool of himself over a woman who had been engaged to another and, in the end, had chosen that man over him.

He'd lived through worse. The death of his parents. The death of his twin's first wife, whom he'd been half in love with all his growing-up years. The end of his rodeo career when he'd caved in several ribs and been advised by the doc to hang up his spurs. Yeah, life was tough.

Hearing steps behind him, he stopped the useless introspection and turned his head.

"I thought I would see if I could help," Lyric said.

Her eyes searched his face anxiously, as if she sought something from him. Welcome? Understanding? Forgiveness? She'd come to the wrong place if she thought he had anything left for her.

He stifled the angry words that rushed to his

tongue. "Sure. Bring the sugar bowl and cream pitcher. I'll carry the cups on the tray."

He picked up the walnut tray he'd made in shop class in tenth grade years ago. Part of him was keenly aware of the woman who followed him into the other room.

After the coffee was served, the two seniors went back to their conversation without a hitch, obviously interested in catching up on the other's life since they'd last met twenty years ago. His uncle's face beamed in pleasure, and Lyric's aunt looked ten years younger in spite of the bruising on her face.

A lump came to Trevor's throat. It wasn't often that sentiment caught up with him, but he felt an over-powering love for this man whose heart had been big enough to take in six kids without a complaint, who'd buried his own wife with quiet grief no more than a year later and who'd lost his own daughter and had never known what happened to the child. Footprints and tire marks had indicated someone had taken three-year-old Tink from the scene of the wreck and left with her, but no one was really sure what had happened.

God, how had the kind, loving uncle stood the pain?

By holding on and meeting each new sunrise one day at a time, Trevor knew. Just as *he'd* done last fall and winter until he'd finally confined all the pain, anger and sense of betrayal to the little black box that was his soul. He'd locked it away and learned to live with it. He would keep on doing that.

Finally the group was ready for bed. He brought in luggage for the aunt and though Lyric insisted on getting her own, he determinedly took her larger suitcase and marched into the house. She trailed behind.

Uncle Nick assigned the older guest to the suite at the end of the west wing. The rose-colored room had its own bathroom and sitting area. Lyric was put in the spare room next to it.

Unfortunately his room was next door to hers, and they would have to share the bath across the hall.

Not at the same time, he hastened to add as his libido picked up on this idea. Okay, so there was still a physical attraction. So what? For a brief moment Trevor considered moving to his cousin's old room in the other wing of the house, but knew that was stupid. He wasn't going to let a woman make him run like a startled deer.

After he saw to the aunt's luggage, he carried Lyric's large case next door. She stood by the bed, her eyes taking in the furnishings.

He set the case on the cedar chest at the end of the bed. The words escaped before he fully realized he was going to say them. "So how's your fiancé?" he asked.

She gazed at him with her soft, doe-like eyes. He saw her throat move as she swallowed, then her breasts—those gorgeous full breasts—lifted as she took a deep breath and slowly released it.

"Lyle—" she began, then stopped as unreadable emotions flickered across her face.

The name was a stab in the gut. Lyle and Lyric, as if they were a matched pair, meant for each other.

"Does it matter?" she finally asked in a strained voice.

He shrugged and left the tempting bedroom before he did something he'd regret—like grab her and crush her to him, like make good use of the bed behind them, like beg her to say she was sorry she'd chosen another over him.

And why the hell didn't she wear an engagement ring like other women?

Chapter Two

On shaky legs, Lyric closed the door, then unzipped the smaller of her two cases. She pulled out the red ankle-length nightshirt made like a football jersey with the numeral one printed on it, a gift from her two brothers last Christmas, then sat on the cedar chest, the jersey clutched to her breasts.

Had Aunt Fay lied about her being included in the invitation to the ranch? If not, then it certainly wasn't Trevor who'd asked for her presence. His uncle? The silver-haired rancher had never met her, so why should he?

With lethal humor, she wished she were still lost on the country roads, driving around and around in endless circles going nowhere. Because at the present moment she felt she'd crossed over into the Twilight Zone.

Lifting her chin, she decided she and Trevor would have to make the best of things. Her aunt planned on staying for the rest of the month.

Of course, she could leave Aunt Fay at the Daltons and go back home. But the hill country of Texas was a long way from Idaho. Since her beloved relative refused to fly, Lyric would have to return for her at the end of the month.

Her shoulders slumped. It was Trevor's duty visit to her aunt—at his uncle's insistence—that had started this whole farce. Closing her eyes, she wondered why life had to be so hard. Tears crowded against her eyes. She held on until they eased and she could think again.

She'd foolishly believed that Trevor had been instrumental in inviting her to the Dalton ranch. She'd thought this meant another chance for them and that he wanted it, too. She'd been wrong, terribly wrong.

There were two choices, she decided. She could crawl into a hole inside herself and wallow in self-pity, or she could refuse to be put off by Trevor's lack of welcome and endure. She was good at enduring.

With a sigh she changed to the nightshirt, unpacked her clothes and put them in the maple dresser. Its beveled, triple mirrors reflected her unhappy countenance back at her from several angles. Red streaks on either side of her nose indicated the bruises that would be visible by morning.

They were nothing compared to the bruises on her heart. She recounted the tragedies life had thrown her way the past eighteen months: the putting to sleep of Scruffs, a lovable and loving stray cat she'd taken in fifteen years ago, due to kidney disease; the divorce of her parents after thirty years of marriage; and then the accident in which Lyle, who lived on the next ranch and had been a friend from birth, had been injured.

The tears pressed close again. She'd cried enough this past year and a half to flood the Rio Grande. Her aunt had told her it was time she put the past behind and started over, that she was young and had all the future before her.

Lyric gave a soft laugh, but it wasn't a happy sound. She hadn't felt young in ages.

Except for one delirious three-week period when a rangy, blue-eyed cowboy had visited Austin for the stock sale. Trevor was twenty-eight to her twenty-four. He'd made her laugh with his jokes and teasing. He'd thrilled her with the way he'd stared at her. She'd done the same, both unable to take their eyes off the other. And his kisses…

A shiver ran over her as she remembered their kisses. Even though they'd had to be careful because of his broken ribs, she'd never been kissed like that, had never responded the way she had to him. It had been wonderful…exciting…and terribly confusing.

She'd never felt that way about Lyle. That fact had added to the uncertainty in her, that plus the quarrel she and Lyle had had the previous month.

She'd refused to set a date for the wedding or to wear his ring. Lyle had been angry. Before he'd gone out of town on business, he'd told her to make up her mind about them before he returned. Or else.

She'd told him then that she wasn't sure she could go through with the marriage. She wasn't ready to be tied down.

Tied down. That seemed an odd way to describe what should have been one of the most exciting times in a woman's life. It wasn't until she met Trevor that the doubts became focused and clear as to why she couldn't marry her old friend. She didn't love him that way.

But then there had been the accident. Trevor had been at her house, having dinner with her, her mom and Aunt F̶ ̶ ̶ ̶ ̶ ̶ ̶ ̶ ̶ ̶ ̶ ̶ call came.

"That was Lyle's mother," she'd said to the other three when she'd hung up the phone. "He's been in an accident near San Antonio and is in intensive care. She said I should come to the hospital at once. He's asking for me."

"Who's Lyle?" Trevor had asked.

"Her fiancé," her mom had answered.

Lyric would never forget the shock, the disbelief, then the fury on Trevor's face as he absorbed this news. "Is that true?" he'd asked.

"No, not exactly. Lyle's been out of town on business this past month," she'd said, stumbling over the words, anxious to wipe the anger from his eyes, the disgust now curling his lips, the accusation in the question.

"How convenient," he'd said.

She realized he thought she was a cheat and deceiver of the first order. "We weren't officially engaged. I was supposed to be thinking it over while he was gone."

"One last fling before tying the knot," Trevor had murmured sardonically, his eyes black pools of anger.

"No—"

"We'd better go, Lyric," her mother had interrupted. "The accident sounds serious."

"Yes. We have to go," she'd said to Trevor, knowing she had no choice.

With her aunt hovering anxiously, and Trevor standing as still as a statue, she and her mom had rushed off into the night, arriving at the hospital an hour later.

Lyle's mother had been distraught. A widow with no immediate family, she'd needed them desperately. The doctors had discovered a tumor in her son's head, one that was inoperable. That was why he'd passed out while driving.

"Trevor," Lyric now whispered to the absent cowboy who'd filled her heart with delight for a short time, "how could I have left him then?"

After talking to the doctors and knowing Lyle

would never recover and that his future was very uncertain, she'd known she couldn't desert him.

Trevor had left the state before she could get back to him. It was just as well. She'd been going to ask him to wait for her, but she knew whatever Trevor had felt for her had turned into hatred. She'd seen it in his eyes tonight when he'd given her the ice bag.

Gathering her toiletry case, she admitted she couldn't have done otherwise and lived with herself. Not even for a man who'd made her heart sing could she have turned her back on her friend's need.

Morning came early on a ranch. Lyric wasn't naturally an early riser, but living on her father's ranch had made her one. Last year, after the divorce, her mother had moved to Austin. Lyric divided her time equally between the two homes and had visited frequently with Aunt Fay who also lived in the city.

As administrator of a four-family trust set up by her grandparents and three other couples who were all friends and whose parents had founded an oil company together in the early 1900s, Lyric had had a busy life since college, spending her time approving grants and participating in various charity functions for the trust foundation. It was a job she could do from anywhere on her laptop computer.

Forcing her reluctant body from the comfortable bed, she went into the bathroom to shower. At once her senses were assailed by a familiar aftershave, by the clean smell of balsam shampoo and soap, and by the memory of being enveloped in Trevor's arms.

She'd loved snuggling her nose against his neck and feeling his arms around her, holding her close, as close as his poor injured ribs could take.

At times during the long, dreary winter, she'd ached to crawl into his embrace and rest there, too weary to ever move again. Trevor, her strong, gentle love…

But none of that was to be, she reminded the longing that rose to choke her. As some wise person had observed long ago: you made your bed; you slept in it. Alone.

She pulled off the jersey and stepped into the shower. Twenty minutes later, hair dry and held off her face in a ponytail, wearing jeans, a knit top and a determined smile, she went into the kitchen.

"Good morning, Lyric," her aunt greeted her.

"Did you sleep okay?" Trevor's uncle asked.

She smiled at the two who lingered at the table with coffee and the newspaper. "Good morning, Aunt Fay, Mr. Dalton. Yes, I slept like a log. Your air is much cooler and conducive to sleep up here," she said.

"It's the mountains," the uncle said. "And Mr. Dalton was my father. Everyone calls me Uncle Nick."

"Uncle Nick," she repeated. Spotting mugs on a rack beside the coffeemaker, she poured a cup and sipped the hot brew that was just the way the ranch cook made it in Texas.."Mmm, delicious."

"Trevor left pancakes and sausage in the oven," the uncle told her.

For the briefest second, she hesitated, then she opened the oven door and removed the plate. Perfect golden circles edged by two links of sausage were ready for eating. Her tummy rumbled, reminding her she hadn't had much food the previous day. She'd been too tense and excited to eat.

So much for great expectations.

"There's milk in the refrigerator," Aunt Fay told her, peering over her glasses.

Lyric poured a glass and took it, along with the coffee and food, to the table. The older couple moved newspaper sections to give her room. She ate in silence while they read and exchanged tidbits from the news.

"Trevor and Travis are in the paddock," Uncle Nick told her when she finished. "They're working with some green cutting horses. Do you need to go to the doctor?"

"No, thanks. I'm stiff but everything works." After refreshing everyone's coffee, she donned a hat and sunglasses, then carried her mug outside and ambled over to the wooden railing of the paddock beside the stable.

The man astride a beautiful bay gelding with black tail and mane looked exactly like Trevor. She knew in a glance that it wasn't. "You must be Travis," she said, leaning on the top rail.

"You got it right in one guess," he told her, his

smile brilliant against his tanned face and heartbreakingly like his twin's. "What tipped you off?"

"Your smile is friendly."

He guided the horse around the *longe* post and stopped it near her. "My brother's isn't?"

She wished she hadn't been quite so candid. "Maybe I take things too personally," she finally said in a light tone as if she were only joking.

The stable door opened. Trevor ducked his head and rode into the paddock on a magnificent black stallion.

"Oh," she murmured.

"Beautiful, isn't he?" Travis nudged the gelding closer to the rails as Trevor put the stallion through several routines such as spinning in a circle and backing, then standing beside a gate while his rider opened it. The two, moving as one, rode out into the pasture.

"What's his name?" Lyric asked, gazing after Trevor and his mount.

"Boa's Ebony. Eb for short." Travis glanced toward the pasture, then back at her. "You ride?"

"Does Texas have cactus?" she countered.

"I'll cut you out a sweet little mare," he said and followed his twin into the pasture.

Five minutes later, he returned with a roan mare. Lyric joined him in the stable. She picked out a saddle and waited while Travis outfitted the mare, then he offered her a leg up. She left her coffee mug on a shelf and swung into the well-used saddle, ignoring the pain in sore muscles.

"Feels good," she said.

He nodded. "Let's go." He led the mare outside to where he'd tied his mount.

The mare didn't need guiding. She dutifully followed the gelding along a dirt track across an adjoining meadow.

They were heading toward a tree-lined ridge, Lyric realized. The ridge defined the beginning of forest and hills that rose ever upward. In the distance one peak stood above several others.

"Is that He-Devil Mountain?" she called to her escort.

He followed her line of sight. "Yes. There are seven peaks that form a sort of semicircle along Hells Canyon. He-Devil is the highest at a bit over 9300 feet."

Hearing the staccato beat of hooves, Lyric looked over her right shoulder in time to see Trevor and the big stallion leap the stock fence of the pasture. They made a perfect picture against the brilliant azure of the sky as they sailed over the fence with a foot to spare.

Her heart rose with them and lodged in her throat, making it all but impossible to breathe.

"Trev was quiet for a long time after he returned from the rodeo circuit last October," his twin remarked in a musing tone. "Some of us figured he'd met someone and fallen hard. Was that someone you?"

She tried to smile as if the idea was absurd, but it wouldn't come. "What makes you think that?"

"Vibes. Or maybe it's just that he's quiet again this morning. I don't think your aunt is the cause, so that leaves you."

"There isn't anything between us," she managed to say.

His eyes, as blue as his twin's, narrowed as he studied her. "I think there is."

"He hates me." The words, spoken aloud, were stark.

"Why don't you two talk it over and clear things up?"

"I...I tried. I wrote him."

Travis heaved an audible breath. "Yeah, he's hardheaded. Don't give up on him," he advised.

"I'm only here because of my aunt. She wanted to visit." The lie nearly stuck to her tongue. "Where are we going?" she asked to divert attention to their journey.

"The Devil's Dining Room," Travis said just as his twin rode up.

The stallion pressed close to the mare, crowding between her and the gelding as if establishing his claim. Trevor's booted foot brushed hers. Even that brief contact was enough to send needles of fire along her leg.

She reined the mare away. "There seems to be a pattern of black markings on your ranch." She spoke to Travis, but it was Trevor who answered.

"There is," he said, letting the stallion take the lead while his twin fell in behind them on the gelding. "Your mount and the gelding are both out of a retired stud. The mare will be bred to Eb here when she's ready."

Lyric nodded stiffly. While familiar with all aspects of ranching, breeding and all that it implied were not topics she wanted to discuss with him.

The stallion tossed its head and pranced.

"He wants a run," Trevor called. "You game?"

She considered her aches, but nodded anyway.

"Ready, set, go," Travis yelled behind them.

The mare took off a split second after the stallion did, almost taking her rider by surprise. Lyric leaned forward as excitement gripped her.

The mare and stallion raced side by side across the wide meadow. Their hooves pounded in time with the beat of her pulse as she urged the mare on.

"Yi, yi, yi," she heard Trevor shout, pushing the stallion to a faster pace.

Trevor and the stallion edged forward, outrunning her and the smaller horse. Lyric didn't ask for more. She knew the mare was giving her all. Surprisingly they closed the gap and came abreast of the other two again.

Trevor looked over at her. Her heart did a somersault at the intensity of his stare. Then the larger horse stretched out and left them in the dust.

Lyric pulled up the mare and watched as the magnificent black beast ran like some mythical creature, hardly touching the ground as it flowed effortlessly with the wind. The rider seemed part of the magic, blending every movement with that of the stallion as they made a great circle.

At last, rider and mount, at a canter now, returned to her and the mare. Trevor's twin, she saw, had gone back to the paddock. Without direction on her part, her horse again followed the other one.

They rode for an hour in silence, until they came upon a stream.

"Let them drink," Trevor said.

She loosened the reins so the mare could dip her head into the tiny creek that wound down the ridge. After that, they rode on, heading for the top and coming out on a flat cliff that had a wonderful view of the ranch.

"The Devil's Dining Room," he said, dismounting.

Lyric did the same and ground-hitched her horse when he did. Trevor let her step up on a boulder, then onto a giant flat piece of granite that jutted over the cliff before he climbed up.

When he sat on the ledge and let his legs dangle over the side, she did, too, although not without misgivings.

"This rock has held all the Daltons at once without falling," he told her.

"There's always a first time," she muttered, staring down into the lovely little valley. The ranch house looked like something for a doll from up here.

Gazing west, she observed the peaks spread out into the distance. "In Texas, you said the seven peaks were named for seven devils that used to come over and eat the children of the people here until Coyote changed them into mountains."

"That's the legend," he agreed.

"He-Devil is the tallest. I saw the name on a road sign. Do the others have names?"

"The Devil's Tooth, Mount Ogre, Mount Baal, the Tower of Babel, the Goblin."

"That's five, plus He-Devil. What's the other one?"

He turned those blue eyes on her. Without blinking, he said, "She-Devil."

It was the breeze, playfully tugging at their hats that finally broke their locked gazes and the silent struggle between them.

"Is that what you think of me?" she asked softly, as if by speaking the words that way, the answer might not hurt.

He set his hat more firmly on his head. "Does it matter?"

"Yes."

Glancing at her once more, he shrugged and rose. "Let's just say I don't think much of a woman who kisses one man while engaged to another." He leaped down to the smaller boulder, then to the ground.

Lyric stood on the hunk of granite and contemplated several retorts. None seemed worthy.

"Didn't you get my letter?" she finally asked when she, too, stood on the ground by the boulders.

He nodded without looking at her.

In the letter she'd tried to explain why her mother had thought she was engaged and why she really hadn't been. She tried again. "Lyle and I were at an impasse. He wanted to announce a wedding date. I wasn't sure enough about us to do that. We weren't engaged, not really."

"So you strung him along, then while he was out of town you experimented with me. You must have decided it was real. You stayed with him."

"Because he needed me."

"Yeah," Trevor said with undisguised bitterness. "He needed you, so you stayed."

"Trevor—"

"The car wreck wasn't all that serious, according to the news later that evening. It didn't kill him or maim him or call for a life-or-death operation, did it?"

She hesitated. "No," she said. "It didn't."

"But you stayed with him. Where's your engagement ring?" he demanded, lifting her hand and holding it between them so they could both see her bare finger. He dropped it as if it might contaminate him with something dreadful.

"At home."

"Your mother said you'd set a wedding date. In June, she said."

Lyric stared at him. "You called? When?" She clutched his arm at his nod. "Trevor, when?"

"After I got the letter. Apparently you'd changed your mind about the marriage." He pulled away from her grasp.

"She didn't tell me about the call."

"I told her not to. I didn't figure it would make any difference." He started toward the horses, then paused. "Would it?" he asked. "Would it have made a difference if we'd spoken? Would you have broken the engagement and come to me...if I'd asked?"

She thought of silent, endless nights at the hospital, of days at Lyle's bedside when he went home, him thinking he was going to be all right, that they would marry and produce an heir to the two ranches.

We'll have children right away, he'd said one afternoon toward the end. *Would you rub my head? These damn headaches seem to be getting worse instead of better.*

His mother hadn't wanted him to know the truth. She'd wanted his final days to be happy ones, filled with plans for the future. He didn't seem to realize he was slipping further and further away as feeling began to leave his body.

He hadn't even noticed when he'd closed a car door on his hand. Lyric had been horrified but had managed to hide it as she released his hand and settled him on the terrace before running to the kitchen for a towel and ice to go on his injury.

He'd become more and more docile as the days

wore on, and then he hadn't wanted her out of his sight during the last weeks. She'd slept on a sofa in his room. Often she'd held him propped up in her arms when his breathing became labored and weak. Then one night he'd whispered, "Thank you for loving me."

Those were the last words he spoke. He'd lapsed into a coma and was gone several hours later.

Studying the strong, healthy man who glared at her as he waited for an answer, she sighed and said softly, "No, I couldn't have come then."

His face hardened. "Then why the hell did you come now?"

Chapter Three

Later that morning, Lyric followed Trevor into town. The station wagon still handled just fine. She'd wanted to wait until she returned to Texas to have it fixed, but Trevor and his uncle wouldn't hear of it.

At the local garage—there was only one—Trevor and the owner examined her car and decided to replace the bumper and the used air bags and to smooth out the crinkle in the nose.

"I'll give you my insurance information," she said, digging into her purse for the card.

Trevor shook his head. "There's no need. I caused the accident. I'll take care of the bill."

"But that's what insurance is for," she protested.

"It's my responsibility," he insisted.

The garage owner observed their argument in amusement, then nodded when she finally shut up and let Trevor have his way, since it was clear he wasn't giving up. While the men made the final arrangements on repairs, she stepped on the running board of Trevor's pickup with a little groan. She seemed to be getting stiffer by the minute.

His hands immediately settled at her waist and lifted her into the cab of the truck. Her skin burned as his heat penetrated her clothing and settled deep inside her.

To her shock, she realized she wanted him...really wanted him. Now. This instant. Longing and need entwined all through her. She wanted passion, yes, but she also wanted comforting. She needed his strength. More than that, she needed his tender, loving care.

Not that he would offer it, she admitted. She was foolish to think she would get another chance with him.

"You'd better relax before your face sets that way," he said when they were on their way.

She frowned at him. "Your twin said you were stubborn. I didn't realize how much."

Trevor shrugged. "You ran off the road because I cut you off. I take care of my mistakes."

"Or walk out on them," she added.

He gave her a warning glance that said, "Drop it."

"Isn't that what you did to me? You thought of our time together as a mistake."

"For good reason. I never encroach on another man's territory."

"I'm not a piece of property to be bought and sold. Or fenced off by some possessive male."

"Fine. You're free as a bird as far as I'm concerned."

"Fine," she said, and stared at the road without looking in his direction again.

Instead of taking the road to the ranch, he turned onto another one running alongside the reservoir that formed a long, narrow recreational lake and supplied the town's water. The water reflected the sky.

The valley was cupped protectively in the palm of the surrounding mountains. It looked too peaceful and lovely to be real. For her it wasn't. Sadness gripped her heart.

Get over it, she advised, rejecting self-pity.

Trevor pulled into the parking lot of a lodge that looked new. "I thought we would have lunch here."

Stifling a protest, she got out before he could help her and joined him on a flagstone path to the front steps.

She felt every movement as a separate pain in each muscle of her body. When he took her arm to help her as they climbed to the broad porch, she couldn't help but flinch.

He paused on the wooden planks and studied her face. "Sore?" he asked.

"Everywhere," she replied with a smile and a little

shrug. A mistake, that. The pain was immediate. Her hand went automatically to her left shoulder.

Trevor frowned, then eased the collar of her shirt away from her neck. "The seat belt," he murmured. "The collarbone may be broken. We'll go see Beau." He paused. "You shouldn't have ridden this morning. If you'd been thrown, your injuries could have been compounded. And serious."

"I wasn't, so I'm fine," she said stoically. "I don't need to see a doctor."

He stared into her eyes like Diogenes searching for one honest person. "Let's go eat," he at last said huskily.

"This is lovely," she said when they entered the soaring, two-story lobby. A huge fireplace was filled with fragrant pine and cedar boughs, ready for a spark to set it flaming. She imagined snow outside, the warm fire inside and a lazy afternoon of lying on the sofa and reading.

Images sprang to her mind of a couple taking their ease there, then laying their books aside and turning to each other, unable to stand another moment without touching.

Lyric sighed shakily and forced the mental scene away. Trevor still held her arm. Using gentle pressure, he guided her into the dining room.

"Lovely," she repeated when they were seated. Their window had a view of the lake and the mountains. "The lodge is new, isn't it?"

He nodded. "We opened a couple of months ago."

"It belongs to you?"

"To the family. My brothers and I, plus our three cousins, put up the money and did most of the construction this past year. The logs came from the ranch. We cut and milled the lumber ourselves."

"My family worked together on the ranch. It was fun." She fell silent, recalling her parents' divorce last year. The shock of it. The bewilderment that thirty years could go down the drain without explanation.

With all their children out of the nest—Lyric was working and had her own place while one brother was a college junior and the other a freshman—their parents had called it quits. They'd admitted the marriage had been in trouble for a long time but they'd concealed it until the youngest child graduated from high school before going their separate ways. The boys had been just as shocked as Lyric.

So much for romantic illusions. She wasn't sure she believed anyone lived "happily ever after" anymore. Two of her friends from school had already split after less than three years of marriage.

She let out a ragged breath composed of equal parts dismay and disillusionment. She really had been foolish to traipse all the way to Idaho chasing after a dream.

Trevor gave her a piercing glance, then his eyes went back to the menu the hostess had given them. The waitress brought the tall glasses of iced tea they'd requested, took their orders and quietly left.

"So why was your mother living in Austin?" he asked. "I thought they were divorced."

What had they been talking about? Oh, yes, her family. "They were. They are. Last year."

She sipped the cool tea, worry eating at her. She hated for things to go wrong. Her aunt said she was too soft-hearted. She didn't know about that, but problems bothered her until she found solutions.

A wry smile settled briefly on her mouth. Perhaps she wanted the standard fairy-tale ending too much.

"Tell me the truth," she requested. "Did you ask your uncle to include me in the invitation to the ranch?"

His eyes reflected the brilliant blue of the lake and sky. "No."

Well, she'd asked. Just to be sure. Just so there wouldn't be any lingering hope on her part.

Her throat tightened so that it was difficult to swallow or to speak. She nodded and smiled at the man who watched her with the fierce stare of a hawk. His gaze held none of the warmth or humor or desire of last fall.

She considered telling him about the final days of winter and that she couldn't have come to him in April or May or June while the grief over her lifelong friend was still so strong. They'd set June the fifteenth as the wedding date. She'd had to get past that first.

However, one look at Trevor's harsh expression told her he wasn't ready to listen, and she couldn't bring herself to plead for his understanding. So she would leave at the end of the month with her aunt.

But if the attraction blossomed again, some part of her added, then perhaps she and Trevor could talk and sort out their feelings. In the meantime, she wanted him to know she wasn't there under any pretenses.

"I'm not engaged, Trevor," she said softly, "not since early in March."

"Another sucker bites the dust," he muttered with a sardonic snort of laughter.

Lyric turned toward the scene outside the restaurant. She studied the view until the swift tempest of emotion passed and the pieces of her heart were pasted together once more. She wouldn't try to explain the past to him again. She just wouldn't.

When the waitress brought their meal, they ate in silence and left immediately thereafter.

"Trevor, hello," a feminine voice called.

Trevor spotted the neighboring rancher's daughter. He'd been going to see her last night when he'd run Lyric off the road. "Hey, Jane Anne," he called.

She crossed the parking lot, then hesitated when she saw he was with another woman. "Hi," she said to Lyric.

Trevor introduced the two women. "Lyric and her aunt are here for the month." He explained about the accident.

"Are you okay?" Jane Anne asked.

Lyric nodded.

The rich brown of her hair picked up shades of auburn and golden amber in the sunlight, he noted. The gold of her eyes flashed when she glanced from him to the other woman. Her face was tanned, her cheeks rosy. Her smile was warm and friendly.

By contrast, Jane Anne looked pale. Her hair was blond, almost white, inherited from Scandinavian ancestors. Her eyes were light blue, her skin very fair. Her smile was cautious. Jane Anne was only eighteen and had graduated from high school in May. In June she'd been dumped by her longtime boyfriend for a girl he'd met in college.

Trevor had started seeing her out of sympathy, his attitude that of a big brother since he was ten years older than she was. "We'll have to think of something to entertain Lyric and give her a sample of mountain hospitality. She's from Texas."

"I have a suggestion," Jane Anne told them. "I was thinking of having a barbecue. I thought you could help me with it," she said to Trevor, giving him a somewhat flirty glance, which startled him. "Let's do it Friday night. We can introduce your guest to the local men."

A spark of something very like jealousy shot through Trevor. He shrugged it off. What Lyric did was nothing to him. They'd had a few laughs, that was all.

Okay, so the last laugh had been on him. He could live with it. He *had* lived with it and gotten over it.

"Great idea," he said. "What time?"

"Around seven-thirty?"

"That'll give me time to help Travis with the chores, so that'll work out."

"I'll call him and Alison. Also Janis and Keith. I want them to come, too."

Trevor nodded. After Jane Anne said her farewells and went inside the lodge, he glanced at his guest. "Alison is married to my twin. Janis is her sister. Janis is married to Keith. He and his partner own the ranch to the north of our place and are running one of those paramilitary camps that are popular now."

Lyric nodded. "I remember you mentioning them."

"Yes." He'd told her all about his family the three weeks he'd been in Texas. They'd laughed at his tale of all the weddings that had been going around like a rash.

Yeah, funny. He'd even thought he'd be among the married men before the year was over. Man, he had gone off the deep end.

But no more.

When he'd learned she was engaged—sort of, according to her story—he'd felt he'd been blindsided by an invisible giant with a club. His heart had been flattened.

An echo of pain chimed someplace deep inside him. He set his jaw and ignored it. He was nearly a year older and a hell of a lot wiser. "Let's go," he said.

Her smile disappeared while her eyes searched his

as if looking for his deepest secrets. He stalked around the pickup and got in, cranking the engine after she did the same and was buckled up. They returned to the ranch without another word.

His uncle was waiting for them to return. "Beau came out during his lunch hour and checked Fay over. He left some pills in case you two gals get to hurting. He said you'll probably feel worse before you're better."

"I think I'll take some," Lyric said.

Trevor looked her over. Damn, he'd forgotten his intention of taking her by the clinic to be checked. He'd noticed she'd moved carefully all morning. A couple of times she'd winced, like when she swung onto the mare up on the ridge. Also when she'd stepped up into the pickup at the garage and again when they'd left the lodge.

Guilt ate at him. He wished he'd been more careful with his driving yesterday. He hadn't, and, as his uncle had often told the kids, there was the devil to pay.

His uncle continued. "Your aunt did, too. She's napping now."

Lyric smiled at the older man. "That was next on my list."

Trevor thought of her in his bed and of holding her while she slept. His body reacted at once. When she recovered from the accident, he could imagine lots of enjoyable things to do in bed.

But not with a woman who responded passionately to one man while thinking of marriage to another.

* * *

Lyric woke slowly, groggily. The knock came again, and she realized that was what had roused her. Glancing at the window, she saw the sky was brilliant with the colors of sunset. "Yes?" she called, sitting up with an effort.

The bruise on her left shoulder where the seat belt had dug in was bluish purple.

"Uncle Nick sent you some salve," Trevor said.

She went to the door and opened it.

He handed over a tube of cream. "Rub it in good. We use it on the horses when they get a sore leg. It seems to work." His grin was wry.

"Thank you. I'll try it."

"Dinner's in about ten minutes."

She nodded. After closing the door, she used the salve on her shoulder and knees. Her skin tingled, then heat spread throughout the sore places. It felt so good, she smoothed the cream over her shoulders and the calves of her legs, too. The scent of camphor, peppermint and cinnamon engulfed her.

After changing from her rumpled clothing to blue slacks and a long-sleeved white silk blouse, she freshened up, then went to the living room. The two men were putting the finishing touches to the table in the dining room. Her aunt was already seated there.

"Join us," the older man said, welcome in his smile. "We were getting worried when you didn't show up all afternoon. You must have needed the rest."

Her eyes burned with sudden tears at his kind tone. Lyric blinked them away as rapidly as they formed, horrified that she might cry in front of them. She sat opposite her aunt while the two men sat at each end of the table.

"I don't recall ever having a three-hour nap. It must have been the pills. I feel great now," she lied.

Trevor made a low sound of disbelief.

Raising her chin, she dared him to dispute her word. He didn't, but his eyes were cynical as he passed a basket of rolls to her.

"What did you think of the mare you rode this morning?" Uncle Nick asked.

"She was smooth and well behaved."

"We're going to breed a championship line from her and the stallion."

"Show horses?"

"Cutting ponies," the uncle corrected.

"That's why you bought the stallion when you were at the stock show," she said to Trevor.

He nodded. "To introduce new blood. Zack wanted to develop a line closer to the Thoroughbreds. He wants them a little taller and quicker than our present stock."

She knew the Seven Devils cow ponies were well-known in ranching circles. "You already raise the best in the West."

His uncle beamed. "Yes, but we can't rest on our laurels. The rancher across the creek is determined to beat us at the state fair next year."

"Is that Jane Anne's father?" she asked.

"Yep," the uncle said. "That girl is a crackerjack rider, too. She wins any competition she enters."

Lyric's heart dropped a couple of inches. Ah, well, one couldn't be the best at everything, she consoled herself.

Smile and be nice for three weeks, that was all she had to do to get through this awkward period with grace. She could do that. Smile and hold the tears inside as she'd done all fall and winter...

Uncle Nick broke into her introspection. "How about a game of Fantan?" he asked. "Do you ladies feel up to it?"

"I do," her aunt declared.

Lyric nodded as three pairs of eyes looked her way. They played cards until ten o'clock. After that, Trevor turned on the television so they could check the news and weather report.

"Clear tomorrow," he said. "Trav and I are going to cut hay before the weather changes."

The local channel came on after the national news. The anchor reported an accident on the highway that had killed a man returning to Boise after a business trip. The camera focused on a woman holding a baby while a little girl clung to her skirts. The little family looked scared.

Lyric pressed a hand to her throat as a terrible ache settled there. She felt their fear and bewilderment, the disbelief that this tragedy could be happening to them. They seemed so alone—the woman, the child and the baby, standing there in front of a little house, the glare of the camera lights catching every nuance of emotion.

Tears, horrible and hurting, flooded her eyes and poured down her face.

"Lyric, honey," her aunt said.

She shook her head. "It's just...they look so sad," she said, trying to explain. She stood. "I'm all right." She rushed from the room.

In the neat bedroom she closed the door and lay down with her hot, streaming face pressed into the pillow.

Nothing like making an utter fool of yourself, she scolded, but the tears wouldn't stop. She'd held them too long...through the turning of leaves in the fall, the rains and ice of winter storms, the blooming promise of a spring that never came. Spring would never come for Lyle, her oldest friend, the playmate of her youth.

But he'd seen the opening of the daffodils and the brilliant show of the tulips. That had made him happy.

The tears continued, each one a separate ache as memories unreeled like a movie—picnics by the river, climbs along the Pedernales River cascades, games of Kick the Can at twilight with cowboys and the ranch children joining in.

She'd loved it all, had reveled in life and its great and wonderful freedom. So had her brothers. So had Lyle.

Sobs shook her body. Grief took her to the far shore

of despair. She'd wanted so much for everything to stay the same, locked in its perfect little niche of happiness.

But her mother had wanted to leave her father; her old friend had wanted more than friendship; and a stranger had entered her idyllic world, forcing her to face its imperfections. Lyle's car wreck had been the final blow to her fantasy.

The woman with the little girl and the baby must have thought her world was perfect, too. She'd baked a cake for her husband's birthday. That was why he was rushing home, so they could celebrate together.

The tears soaked the pillow, their supply seemingly endless. Lyric willed them to stop, but they wouldn't.

The air stirred, and faint light brightened the room for a second as the door opened, then closed. She heard the footsteps on the oval braided rug. Not her aunt. Trevor.

"Lyric?" he said in that uncertain way men had when confronted with an emotional woman.

"Go away," she said. "Please. Go away."

"I can't."

He sat on the side of the bed, then leaned close. His big hand stroked down her hair, stripping away the band that held it in place so he could run his fingers through the strands.

"Don't," he murmured.

"I c-can't h-help it." Each word was whispered on a sobbing breath, like a child trying to hold the tears back but unable to.

She felt him release a deep breath as he bent close to her temple. His lips touched her there ever so gently.

"Your aunt said you'd been unhappy for a long time. She said I should ask you to tell me about it."

Lyric shook her head and kept her face pressed into the pillow. The tears were never going to stop, not in a hundred years, and she wasn't going to share any tales of woe with a man who hated her for deceiving him.

He shifted until he stretched out beside her. He rubbed her scalp and her back, massaged along her spine. "Then cry, if you have to, until the tears are gone."

A fresh flood ensued at his words. He silently waited for her to finish. After a long time, she became aware of his heat along her right side. She realized that deep within she was cold in spite of the hot tears. She moved closer.

She felt his hesitation, then he laid a leg over both of hers. Lifting her hair, he kissed the back of her neck and along her blouse collar.

"You smell so good," he said. "Like ambrosia. You remind me of days spent working in the sun, the scent of summer in the air. Of coming to the house and finding my favorite cake cooling in the kitchen, the aroma making my mouth water. You make me hungry for things that used to be."

Lyric felt his words sift down to her soul, saw them as sun motes that danced in the air. Need and longing stirred in her, blending all the unspoken desires of her heart into one yearning. She turned to her back so she could study him in the faint glow of an outside light.

"Are you feeling sorry for me?" she asked.

He shook his head. "I don't know. Maybe for both of us. And Lyle." He gave a half laugh that sounded infinitely sad. "The other point in this odd triangle."

She lifted one hand and pushed back the stubborn lock of hair that fell over his forehead. His uncle's was the same, she'd noted. A family trait.

Tears filled her eyes again.

He brushed them off her lashes with his finger, then he kissed the moisture off her cheeks. "Tell me what's wrong."

As sudden as the tears had appeared, passion took their place, rushing through her in a great tidal wave of hunger that had been suppressed much too long. Gazing into his eyes as he tried to understand her outburst, she knew they were too vulnerable at this moment to stay in the room alone.

Knew it, but didn't stir, didn't suggest they go.

She laid her hands on his chest and soaked in the warmth there. She touched his throat, followed the strong cords of his neck, explored his jaw where muscles quickly contracted and relaxed.

Running her fingers into his hair, she cupped his head between her hands. With the lightest of pressure, she brought his face closer to hers. She felt his breath on her lips. She opened her mouth, licked her lips. He did the same. They were ready for the kiss.

Forever after, in all the seasons of all the years to come, she would have to acknowledge she had been the one to make the final move.

Slowly, savoring the moment, she touched her mouth to his. That was all it took.

The shudder that ran through him entered her and sent a tremor all the way to her toes. She pushed her sandals off and wrapped her legs around his. He pulled her closer, rolling so he half lay on her.

Hunger, so great it overlaid the earlier grief that had filled her, became an unreasonable force inside her. She tugged at his shirt until it was free of his jeans, then moved away enough so that she could unfasten the buttons.

His hands closed over hers. "What are we doing?" he asked, his voice dropping a register.

She shook her head slightly, negating the question. "Don't talk," she whispered. She pushed the shirt off his shoulders, her hands feverish now, restless with the need that drove her past thought and spoken words.

"Lyric—"

Biting at his lips, she silenced him with kisses and passionate nips until he crushed her mouth under his, demanding entry so that they shared the kiss fully.

It took only seconds to tug the snap on his jeans, to slide the zipper down. He rolled away enough to unfasten the pearl buttons of her blouse, to loosen and push her slacks to her hips. She raised her hips and felt the air caress her bare skin as the slacks and the tiny lace thong slid from her to the floor. Her blouse and bra followed.

He kicked free of his pants and briefs, then affixed protection. When he came back to her, they touched skin to skin from their lips to their toes. He fingered her breasts until the nipples rose in tight buds of passion.

"Yes," she murmured. "Yes."

"I don't know why we're doing this—"

She laid fingers over his lips. "Don't think," she begged. "Don't...don't go away."

He gazed at her with such desire in his eyes she knew her request was unnecessary. "Do you think I could?"

The question needed no answer. His body was a pulsating hardness against hers. She opened her thighs and pressed against that rigid strength as he settled over her. His groan was low and sexy, thrilling her with his hunger.

"I've never wanted this way," she told him, running her hands over every inch of him that she could reach. "Never needed...not like this."

"It's never been like this," he agreed, his voice a delicious growl in her ear.

He kissed a tender spot there, then sucked on her earlobe before returning to her mouth. With a gentleness that surprised her, he explored her breasts, her abdomen, her hips, then touched her intimately, drawing a gasp as passion flamed anew.

Lifting his hand, he tasted the dew of her body, then touched her lips so she could taste, too.

"I want to know you completely," he said.

When he slipped downward, she closed her eyes and tried to breathe, but air wasn't necessary. She could live just by holding him and feeling his sweet, sweet caresses.

With tenderness and patience, he showed her how intimate they could be, how brightly passion could flare between them, how fire could be liquid and lightning could flow through her veins.

"Oh," she murmured, a warning in the word as he took his fill of her. "Oh," she said again.

He rose, his arms braced on either side of her. Gazing into her eyes, he melded them into one.

"Trevor," she said on an almost silent cry as the need became unbearable. "Yes, oh, yes, oh, yes...yes."

She felt the tremors move from her to him, then his lips were on hers again, his tongue moving with each thrust of his body. They both stopped breathing. She felt another wave of sensation flow over her at the same moment she sensed his throbbing release. Saying his name on a sob, she spun away into eternity....

For many moments there was only the sound of their breathing as they lay side by side, still joined. She smoothed the stubborn lock off his forehead and managed a smile as contentment urged her to close her eyes and let sleep take her.

"Am I a substitute for your former fiancé?" he asked.

The words struck deep, a separate barb in each one. "He died," she whispered past the pain. "That's why I couldn't come to you. He was ill, and then he died."

She felt every muscle in his body go stiff, then he tore himself out of her arms and out of the bed. He gathered his clothing into a ball.

"I won't take another man's place," he told her, "not even a dead one's."

He walked out. In a minute she heard the shower come on. Later she heard him leave his room. He wore boots, so she knew when he left the house.

The tears, which she'd thought were endless, didn't come to wet her dry, burning eyes.

Chapter Four

Friday night Trevor drove the ranch station wagon to the cookout at the neighbor's spread. Lyric sat up front in the passenger seat, feeling like an interloper. The tension sizzled between them, but Travis and Alison, in the back seat, didn't seem to notice it.

"I'm nervous," Alison confided. "This is our first outing since Logan was born."

Lyric glanced behind her in time to see Travis hug his wife of fourteen months. He spoke softly to her, "Rest easy. Uncle Nick and Lyric's aunt are in heaven because they are going to take care of him."

"Yes, but will they still be happy by the time we get home?" Alison's smile was rueful. "If he cries the whole evening, your uncle may never baby-sit again."

"No problem," Trevor said. "Uncle Nick has a special way with babies. At church all the kids want to sit with him."

Lyric, glancing at his handsome profile, thought of Trevor with a child. He'd brought the four-month-old into the house, his touch gentle and sure, and laid the infant into his uncle's waiting arms. She had no doubt that he would make a good father.

The ever-present gloom shrouded her spirits, and she turned her thoughts to the evening ahead. She'd never felt less like socializing. However, she dredged up a pleasant expression when they stopped before a white frame house, mostly Victorian in style.

The two couples were met by Jane Anne. Lyric held on to her smile as Trevor and Jane Anne kissed lightly. The younger woman welcomed her with a hug and did the same with Alison and Travis. "We're all out back," she told them.

Leading the way through a wide hall, she ushered them to a deck where several other people were already gathered. There, their hostess introduced Lyric to the group. Of the four couples already there, she recognized the names of Janis and Keith Towbridge. Janis was the younger sister of Alison. Their ranch adjoined the Dalton spread.

"What did you do with K.J.?" Alison asked the couple.

"Left the little monster with Jonah," Janis answered.

Keith patted his wife's shoulder at her rueful description of their year-old son. "The monster is teething and not very happy about it. Jonah is a brave man."

Another couple chimed in with remedies for teething toddlers while Jane Anne led Trevor to a gas grill at one corner of the deck. Giving him a spatula, she put him to work cooking several large steaks and chicken pieces on skewers with pineapple.

Lyric realized that she was the odd person in this get-together. All the rest were paired off, and it was clear to her that Jane Anne considered Trevor her partner. Self-conscious about being alone, she settled in a cushioned patio chair and pushed a determined smile on her face. There she sat for the next hour, speaking only when Alison thoughtfully brought her into the general conversation.

At last the dinner was ready. The two rectangular patio tables had enough room for six people each. A round table had four chairs, but no one was sitting there.

Lyric hesitated, not knowing where she was supposed to go. There were two empty chairs at the table nearest the grill, but three people were still standing. Trevor, Jane Anne and herself.

"Zack and Honey are supposed to be here," Jane Anne said, "but he's working late. They still plan to come when he's through."

"Scoot over, honey," Alison said to Travis. "Come on, Lyric, you can sit beside me. Bring your chair."

"I'll get it," Trevor said. "There's plenty of room on this end for another person."

He moved a chair to the end of the table, seated Lyric, then took the chair beside her. That left Jane Anne with the chair to his right at the side of the table.

The younger woman looked annoyed for a second, then she joined them and began to pass the platters and baskets of delicious smelling food.

Lyric found she actually was hungry. She hadn't eaten much yesterday or today. She hadn't wanted anything, not since her blissful tryst with Trevor ended so disastrously. Except at meals, he had avoided her completely while he worked in the hay fields, baling feed for the cattle to last the long cold winter.

A chill crept through her, as if the Snow Queen sent her a foretaste of the season ahead.

Taking a kabob of chicken, she concentrated on the dinner. With several kinds of chips and salsa, the meal was delicious, reminiscent of those they served at her home in Texas. Hot rolls were crusty on the outside while the corn and tomato salsa was fresh and spiced just right.

"Do you give out your recipes?" she asked Jane Anne. "I would love to have the one for this salsa."

Her hostess burst out laughing. "You've caught me. It's from the grocery in town. They have a bakery and deli where they make lots of take-out stuff. Most everything came from there."

As the others laughed, Lyric realized she was the only one who hadn't known the food wasn't home-made. She felt heat spread up her neck and into her face. Fortunately the lighting was dim and intimate on the deck, so she didn't think anyone noticed. "I'll check with them, then."

Glancing to her right, she met Trevor's gaze. He observed her as if she were an alien from some for-eign universe, then looked away. Outsider, his gaze said.

Loneliness speared through her while the sadness of winter and spring returned like a haunting dream.

Three weeks, she reminded herself. Anyone could hold out for three weeks.

She swallowed a bite of chicken, then another. Smiling, answering when spoken to, she got through the long evening without a break in her composure.

Just as the meal was completed, they heard a car engine out front. "That must be Zack and Honey," Trevor said.

It was. The last couple joined them, apologizing for the delay as Jane Anne served them from platters that still contained loads of food. They ate hungrily.

"Were you on a case?" their hostess asked.

Zack nodded. "Actually more of the same-old, same-old from last year." He glanced at the twins, then at Keith. "A steer slaughtered over near your place. Your partner said the play soldiers hadn't been out that way."

"That's right," Keith said, nodding. "We've been

careful to make sure they know the boundaries of our ranch. Paint balls don't usually carry a killing punch.''

The wry remark brought chuckles from the men. Lyric gathered that Keith and his partner catered to paramilitary types who liked to play at war, shooting each other with paint balls to indicate a strike.

"Did you find any clues?" Trevor asked his brother.

Zack looked glum. "Not much. Some indistinct prints, oh, and this." He pulled an object from his pocket. "I have no idea if it's a clue or not."

With the rest, Lyric peered at a pink plastic barrette shaped like a bow. "A child's," Jane Anne said.

"A little girl's," Alison said at the same time.

"It doesn't make much sense," Zack told them. "What would a kid be doing with someone slaughtering a steer? The barrette was probably lost during a family backpacking trip last month. Or even last year."

Lyric didn't think the timing was right. The bow had no encrusted dirt that indicated it had been exposed to the elements very long. She kept her opinion to herself.

"It's too clean to have been there long," Trevor said.

"Yeah." The deputy shook his head. "This case looks the same as the four we had last year. The slaughter stopped during the winter, though."

Trevor snorted. "No rancher in his right mind leaves his cattle in the hills in winter."

The others burst into laughter, reminded that no rustler in his right mind would be out in winter, either.

"So someone comes up and lives off the land, so to speak, in the summer, you think?" Travis asked.

Zack shrugged and finished off the last bite of steak, the last chip and the last bit of salsa on his plate. He eyed his wife's remaining portion of chicken. She handed it over with a long-suffering sigh that brought another round of merriment from the group.

Lyric's eyes were drawn to Trevor at this display of married compatibility. A muscle jerked in his jaw, but he didn't glance her way.

For a short time that spring, after her aunt delivered the invitation, she'd thought there was a chance for them. She'd dreamed of it, had wanted it more than anything, but that daydream had truly passed.

Lifting her glass, she sipped the iced tea and tried not to remember what once was and what might have been.

After the meal, she'd hoped they would go home, but their hostess had other things in mind. Loading a CD player, Jane Anne tugged Trevor to his feet and to the middle of the deck. When the music began, they danced.

Four couples joined them.

Lyric sat with Travis, Alison, Zack and Honey. Both women were cordial to her and included her in their talk of the community. Honey had been a professional dancer before her marriage and taught classes in town. She was in charge of an effort to raise funds for new sound equipment at the local community center.

"It's a musical," she explained. "Do you happen to dance, sing or play a musical instrument?"

"No, sorry," she told the slender, graceful blonde.

"But," Trevor drawled, moving his dance partner closer to the table, "she does head up a charitable foundation that gives grants for things like that. Can the money be used out of the state of Texas?" he asked her, standing in one place and mostly swaying to the music.

Lyric nodded. "Most of it has to go to local endeavors, but a percentage can be used outside the state." She spoke to Honey, "Would you like me to send you the forms?"

Honey nodded, her eyes shining. "We'll have to get Seth and Amelia to fill them out."

"Seth is our lawyer cousin. Amelia is his wife. They're the business brains in the family," Travis told Lyric.

"I remember Trevor mentioning them."

She remembered everything he'd told her about his fascinating family during his stay in Austin. They had talked incessantly between the hot, sweet, much-too-tempting kisses. Her lips tingled at the memory.

Deep-blue eyes met hers, and she knew Trevor was recalling their time in Texas and all that had happened between them. She'd shared family stories with him, too…everything but the fact that she was supposed to be thinking of marriage to another man.

He moved away, twirling his partner in time to the music, condemnation in his eyes.

Lyric stared at the dark horizon and the many stars that glowed in the night sky. Millions, billions of worlds out there, and she had to be born on this one.

With an inward grimace at the self-pitying thought, she turned back to the amiable group and listened while the discussion returned to the mysterious cattle rustlers or whatever they were.

Lyric considered the pink barrette and what it might mean. Assuming the girl's parents were caught killing cattle, they could go to jail. The girl would be put in a foster home or sent to a state correctional center. Life could be so terribly hard for children.

Not that it was any of her business. She wouldn't be here long enough to get involved. Not with anything. She glanced at Trevor as he leaned over his partner in a deep dip at the end of the dance. Not with anyone, she added.

A slow love song started. The two couples at the table rose, then Lyric saw Alison and Travis hesitate when they realized she would be alone. "Go on," she encouraged them. "I'm too sore to dance."

Actually she was much better than she'd expected. Uncle Nick had insisted she and her aunt use ice packs several times on their knees and noses and, as they'd belatedly discovered, their collarbones. The bruises on each side of her nose were already pale magenta and green instead of purple, a definite improvement.

After a couple of minutes of watching the others, she heard a phone ring inside the house. Jane Anne's mother called to her daughter. When the girl went inside to answer, Trevor came over to the table.

"Do you want to dance?" he asked.

"No, thanks."

He settled into the chair beside her. Turning it sideways to the table, he stretched out his long legs, then covered a yawn.

"You were up early," she began, then stopped, not wanting to appear as if she kept track of him.

"The haying," he murmured and patted back another yawn.

"We should go home so you can go to bed—"

His eyes swung to her with a dangerous glint, cutting off the unwise flow of words. "Yeah," he said coolly. "I'll tell Jane Anne we're leaving."

With that, he went into the kitchen. Lyric stood and waited. Inside, she could hear Trevor's voice, then laughter from the couple, then silence. And silence. And silence.

She tried valiantly not to think about what they might be doing, but it was useless. She imagined a long sweet kiss growing into passion…

"Ready?" Trevor asked, appearing at the door.

She nodded.

"Are you two leaving?" Alison asked.

"Yeah," Trevor told her. "Can you and Trav get a ride with Janis and Keith?"

"No problem," Keith called out.

Alison nodded. She asked Trevor and Lyric to dinner Saturday night so she and Lyric could get acquainted.

"Great," Trevor said with false heartiness.

On the ride home Lyric spoke, "Don't feel you have to entertain me or…or escort me to any more parties at your friends' homes."

He cut her a sideways glance. "Bored? Our night life here doesn't compare with Austin's."

"That isn't it." She stared at the stars and felt as remote and insignificant as those pinpricks of light against the night sky. "I was forced on you. I think that was my aunt's doing. I'm sorry."

He heaved an audible sigh. "My uncle was probably in on the scheme. He loves nothing better than to coax us along in our love lives. Has he told you to seduce me yet?"

"No," she said, shocked at the idea.

"He will." Trevor parked in front of the horse rail and turned off the engine. He sat there with his hands resting on the steering wheel. "You can tell him you already tried that…and it didn't work."

He got out of the vehicle, slammed the door and walked off into the night. Lyric sat there for another minute, her gaze on the peaks to the west of the ranch. He-Devil Mountain rose above the other peaks, remote and majestic and untouchable.

Realizing a great fatigue, she went into the ranch house. Before she closed the door, she heard the impatient dance of hooves on the turf and turned in time to see Trevor and the stallion leap the fence and ride off into the night.

She thought of the three weeks they'd had last fall. A person could live a lifetime in three weeks.

"Come join me," Aunt Fay invited, upon seeing Lyric at the door Saturday morning. "You slept late. Was the barbecue fun?"

Her aunt sat on the front porch, a ranch magazine in her lap. Lyric went outside. The sun was warm but not yet hot. She glanced all around but didn't see anyone else.

"Yes, it was. The food was delicious. Jane Anne said it was from a deli in town. We'll have to try it."

"Mmm," her aunt said.

"How are your bruises?"

"Much better, although I'm a bit stiff in the getting-up-and-down department. You seem to be recovering quickly."

"Yes." Lyric surveyed the ranch again. "Where is everyone?"

"In the hay field. Rain is predicted tonight."

Lyric looked to the southeast. Texas storms often came in from the Gulf in the summer. But this wasn't Texas. Turning to the west, she saw dark clouds obscuring the line of peaks.

"Aunt Fay, why did you let me think I was invited to the ranch with you?"

"You were. Nicholas knows I don't fly and that the drive was too long for me to come alone. He said they had lots of room if I wanted to bring someone."

"But you knew what happened, that Trevor and I...and then the accident..."

"I know that you've grieved enough. It's time you got over feeling guilty about Lyle. You were a good friend to him. The fact that he wanted more wasn't your fault. You were honest with him," her aunt concluded firmly.

"Trevor thinks I cheated on Lyle."

"Dalton men have hard heads."

Lyric managed a smile. "And hearts," she added.

Aunt Fay shook her head. "Not their hearts, Lyric. They're as tender as spring grass there. You just have to find a way past the protective barriers." She smiled encouragement at her niece. "You can do that."

"You're a romantic," Lyric scolded mildly.

"Yes. Perhaps it's a failing of mine. At any rate, I don't want you to lose this chance at happiness."

Lyric thought the odds were against it, but she didn't say so. "Did you lose someone you loved once?"

Aunt Fay studied her for a moment before answering. "Like Lyle, I wanted more than was offered. Nicholas Dalton took one look at my cousin and fell in love. It was the same for her. Although I met him first, I knew when to step aside gracefully and retain some dignity."

Lyric was stricken by this news. "I'm sorry. I didn't know. Is that the reason you never married?"

"No," the older woman said with some asperity. "I didn't marry because no one asked. However, I led a busy life, especially after your grandparents died and your father came to live with me. I had a family and a ranch to take care of. It was quite enough."

"Oh."

Her aunt laughed. "I was never the idealist that you are, child. You think the world should be perfect. I always knew it wasn't."

"Well, I'm learning," Lyric declared ruefully.

Her aunt hesitated, then added, "Don't give up your dreams without a struggle. That's why I wanted you here. Nick and I, interfering old fools that we are, wanted you and Trevor to have this chance."

Lyric couldn't bring herself to explain how hopeless it was in light of her favorite relative's belief that all would work out. She knew who was the pragmatist and who was the idealist in the family.

Trevor washed up at the barn sink, then hurried to the house. He was the last one in due to driving the last load of cured hay to the storage barn, and he was hungry.

The scent of roasting meat made his mouth water as he entered the ranch house. He stopped halfway to the dining room. Lyric, carrying a platter of roasted potatoes and carrots, stopped, too.

"Uh, lunch is ready," she said and hurried on.

He followed her to the table. His uncle was already there. A fifth plate was set.

"Zack called. He'll be here…ah, that must be him now," Uncle Nick said.

Trevor heard the truck stop and the engine die, then the slam of the cruiser's door. Zack was a deputy sheriff and drove the standard issue SUV from the department. In this country, they needed the four-wheel-drive vehicle.

"Be there in a sec," Zack called upon entering. In a minute he joined them at the table after washing up in the bathroom Trevor and Lyric shared.

"What's happening out this way?" Trevor asked his older brother when everyone was seated.

"A rancher claimed the poachers got another one of his cattle. I checked it out. Looked like old age to me. The coyotes had pretty much destroyed the carcass, so it was hard to tell."

"Any footprints?"

"Not a one, except the rancher's."

"Coyotes," Trevor said, agreeing with his brother's assessment of the situation.

Since Lyric sat on Zack's left, it was impossible to look at his brother and not see her, too. She'd put makeup over the fading bruises on her nose so they were invisible. A bit of color showed along the neckline of her T-shirt, the angry smudge reminding him of his part in her injuries. She also suppressed a grimace each time she rose. Her knees had taken the brunt of the accident.

Guilt caused him to frown just as she glanced his way. Her eyes widened as if she was startled, then she looked back at her plate and kept her eyes there. No expression crossed her face.

Zack noticed him staring at Lyric. "By the way," he said. "Lyric's car will be ready Monday. If you come into town, give Honey a call. We'll meet you for lunch."

When Lyric didn't say anything, Trevor shrugged. "I'll have to see what happens with the weather."

"You need help tomorrow with the hay?" Zack asked, turning to his uncle.

"We wouldn't turn anyone away," Uncle Nick said. "But if the storm comes in tonight, it'll be too wet to do anything tomorrow."

"Well," the lawman said, "I don't have another day off for ten days. We're short of help."

"So what else is new?" Trevor quipped.

"A baby, the doctor says."

"What?" Uncle Nick all but shouted. "You and Honey are going to have a baby?" His grin spread all over his leathery, lined face. "That's the best news I've heard since Travis and Alison said they were expecting. The family is growing at last."

Trevor groaned internally as the old man waxed on and on about the future and everyone settling down and producing the necessary children to ensure the future of the clan. Since he was the only one not yet settled with a wife and possible family, the lecture was obviously for his benefit.

Lyric, he noticed, didn't once look up from the roast and vegetables on her plate. She took a bite every now and then to make it look as if she was actually eating. Taking his cue from her, he ate and didn't say a word during the sermon on the importance of family to a man.

"Tell Honey to remember her vitamins," his uncle concluded in satisfaction. "She's eating for two now."

Trevor's eyes were drawn to Lyric. An image of her carrying his child flashed into his mental vision. At least he'd had the presence of mind to use protection the other night. There would be no rushed marriage because of impending parenthood for them.

Marriage. Man, that would be a disaster in the first degree. He would never forget she'd been engaged for all practical purposes when she'd responded so ardently to his kisses last fall. Women, like the weather, were not to be trusted. Period. He brought his attention back to the table.

"What are you planning on doing this afternoon?" Uncle Nick asked Lyric.

"I—I don't know. I mean, I don't have plans," she said, taken off guard. "I was thinking of taking a ride?" Her voice ended in a question.

"Good idea. Riding always clears the mind for me," the older man said.

"Don't go far," Trevor advised, his tone harsher than he'd meant it to be. "We don't have time to rescue you if you get lost."

Her chin lifted. "Don't worry. I can take care of myself."

Trevor nodded. "Women are like cats," he said in a falsely jocular manner. "They always land on their feet."

"Always," she echoed, her face stubborn and surprisingly defiant as she met his eyes.

Zack raised his eyebrows and gave him an odd smile. "They do make life interesting, though," he murmured.

"Huh," Trevor said to that.

Chapter Five

"Would it be okay if I went for a ride?" Lyric asked Uncle Nick after the luncheon dishes were taken care of and the kitchen cleaned up. She wasn't taking anything for granted in this household.

He checked the sky before answering. "Yes. The rain won't be in until tonight. Follow the dirt road that crosses the pasture and stay straight on it instead of taking the trail up to the Devil's Dining Room. That's a nice ride."

And by staying on the road, she wouldn't get lost, she added silently, deducing the rest of his thoughts on the subject. "Thank you. I'll be gone a couple of hours, so don't worry about me."

It would take a long ride to clear her mind.

"We won't," her aunt said. She turned to the uncle. "Lyric has been riding since she was a toddler. Her sense of direction is excellent."

Uncle Nick nodded. "Keep an eye on the clouds. Storms can come up quick in the mountains. There's a line shack west of the road about an hour and a half from here in case you need shelter. Follow the creek that cuts across the road and you'll find it. The boys keep it stocked."

"Perhaps you'd better take a raincoat," her aunt suggested, looking a bit worried.

"I'll get her one," Uncle Nick said.

Lyric rolled up a rain poncho provided by the elder Dalton and took it with her. She whistled for the mare, tossed on the saddle with only a low moan escaping as she moved her left shoulder, then rode out, picking up the dirt road about halfway across the pasture.

In the paddock next to the stable, the stallion trumpeted and ran along the fence, calling the mare to him.

"Easy," Lyric said, patting her mount's neck as the mare tossed her head restlessly.

She let the horse pick her own easy pace along the dirt track while she enjoyed the scenery. When the road climbed higher and a narrow path cut to the right, the mare started to take the woodland trail, but Lyric gently held her to the road.

Over an hour later, they came to a creek that cut a channel through the forest. A culvert had been laid where it once flowed across the road, and covered with gravel so vehicles could easily cross it. Hmm, the cabin must be near, but she wasn't interested in going there.

She dismounted and let the mare drink her fill from a pool formed at the base of a three-foot waterfall before the creek disappeared into the culvert.

The water looked cool and inviting. She stooped and trailed her fingers through the crystal pool. Framed by the sky, her reflection gazed back at her, the funny bruises on each side of her nose forming streaks under her eyes, rather like a raccoon's markings.

As she rose, a footprint in the dirt next to her boot caught her eye. The print wasn't quite as long as hers. A woman or a young boy.

Or a girl who liked pink barrettes in her hair?

A beat of excitement stirred through Lyric. She bent and studied the print, then searched in a semicircle for others. Just as she was about to give up, she found another print at the side of the road. It pointed in the direction she was going.

Leading the mare, she picked up other prints several feet farther along, the stride longer. The child had been running…ah, here she veered to the other side of the road…and here she left the road to follow a game trail through the trees.

Lyric followed the faint path down the steep slope until it opened onto a mountain meadow spotted with daisies and cornflowers and wild mustard. Her heart lurched as a dark shadow flew over her head.

She followed the buzzard's flight to the far side of the meadow and saw others were gathered there. With a quickening pulse, she mounted and rode over.

The stench of the carcass hit her nostrils before she came to it. A few buzzards circled high overhead and a couple of snarly coyotes slunk into the forest when she arrived. Lyric surveyed what was left of the calf.

It had been killed with one clean hit from a high-powered rifle. The meatiest parts had been removed. Sections of the hide had been cut away, used to wrap the cuts of meat, she assumed. The culprit knew what he was doing.

Or was it a she?

Lyric stared at the familiar footprint in the dust. The girl had been here, too. There were other prints around the carcass, bigger ones, Lyric discovered after a careful search of the area. Whose?

The mare stamped her feet and pranced at the end of the rein. Lyric tightened her hold. She, too, was wary. Besides buzzards and coyotes, bears and pumas were attracted to the scent of carrion. She knew staying in the vicinity could be dangerous, but she wasn't ready to give up. She was worried about the child.

Checking the nearby woods and meadow often for predators, Lyric scouted for more prints. Finding a faint trail into the woods, she followed it on gut instinct. At one point, she thought she smelled wood smoke, but couldn't tell the direction of it. The air was still now, as if holding its breath.

At an opening in the trees, she studied the mountain

peaks. The clouds were darker. They were moving eastward, driven by a high wind that she couldn't detect from her present position.

A sense of urgency invaded her. She bent to her task once more, but couldn't find a clear track. Finally she straightened her stiff back and pushed her hat off her forehead. A gust of wind, suspiciously cool, hit her.

The storm was on its way.

Glancing at her watch, she was startled to see it was late afternoon. Almost six. She'd been gone over four hours. Her aunt would be worried.

"I'll tell Trevor," she murmured to the mare after she was mounted and on her way back. "He'll help me find the little girl."

The mare flicked one ear toward her and kept the other tuned to the west. A faint rumble sounded in the distance.

"Thunder," Lyric said. "I hear it, too."

When they came to the meadow again, she urged the mare to a smooth canter until they reached the slope and started up, then they had to slow down. Upon reaching the dirt road, she again pressed her mount to a faster gait.

Rounding a sharp turn, she came face-to-face with Trevor. He pulled his mount to a halt, his expression grim. Without saying a word he lifted a gun from its scabbard.

After firing off three rounds, he put the rifle away

and sat there without speaking. From the distance came an answering volley of shots.

"Okay, they know you're found," he said. "Let's get back to the house. Your aunt is worried."

"I know," Lyric said in apologetic tones. "I lost track of time."

"Yeah, well, try to remember that the rest of us have work to do. We can't stop and chase you down every time you take a notion to head out on your own."

He wheeled his mount, a roan gelding, in a tight circle and started home.

"Wait!" she called. "I found something." Nudging the mare into a trot, she came up beside him. "There's a carcass...but before that, I found footprints, small ones. I was following those when I saw the buzzards."

Trevor frowned at her. "Start over," he ordered. "And make sense."

A hot streak of anger flashed through her. She began again. "When I stopped to let the mare drink, I spotted a small footprint by the pool. I tracked it down the slope to a meadow. On the far side of that, I found a calf carcass and more footprints. They led to a trail in the woods. I lost the prints there and turned back."

Trevor shot her a look that could have skinned a cat at thirty paces. "If you'd come upon the poachers, what was your next move—a citizen's arrest?"

"I hadn't thought that far ahead," she admitted

honestly. "I was concerned for the child. The little girl—"

"You have no idea if there was a girl," he said in the same controlled, furious tone. "You don't know who or how many were involved. You—"

"There were three of them," she interrupted. When he glared at her, she glared back. "There were three different sets of prints, all of them sneakers, no boots. That makes me think they're all rather young. Teenagers maybe, except for the girl. She's probably ten or so."

"Oh, yeah? Was her age stamped on the sole of her shoe?"

"No, but her foot is smaller than mine. Furthermore, I know what kind of sneakers they were from the sole design. They're a brand popular with the younger girls back home."

The mare moved closer to the gelding as the harsh words flowed between the humans. Lyric reined her mount to the side before her foot could brush against Trevor's. She didn't want any contact with the arrogant male.

He glanced at the sky, then clicked to the gelding to increase their speed. Lyric saw the clouds were gaining on them, swooping in like birds of prey across the treetops. The wind was brisk and growing colder with each gust.

"How far are we from the ranch?" she asked.

"We're on it."

"I meant to the house," she said coldly.

"Another hour."

She shut up. The rest of the trip was accomplished in dead silence, except for the swift beat of the horses' hooves. Finally the trees opened to the pasture. Beyond that, the lights of the ranch house glowed with welcome.

"Home," she said, almost giddy with relief.

"My home."

Not yours, was the rest of that statement.

"I know," she replied. "The Seven Devils Ranch. I'm well acquainted with one of them."

With that, she pulled up at the railing and dismounted. Travis came out of the stable. "I'll take care of the horses," he said. "You two better report in."

"Thanks." Lyric tossed him the reins and stalked off toward the house.

"Uh, better watch it, bro. Looks as if you brought a wildcat back on this trip," she heard Travis say behind her, obviously finding the situation amusing.

"Yeah," Trevor agreed with no humor at all. "Her tail is in a knot, but then so is mine."

She heard his footsteps and speeded up. But the devil behind her stayed right on her heels.

Trevor felt the first drops hit the side of his face and right arm before they'd traveled halfway across the fifty yards between the paddock and the horse rail separating the lawn from the road. He peered toward the west and saw sheets of rain heading their way, driven by the leading edge of the mountain wind that swept over them just then. Mother Nature's calling card.

"Run!" he called.

Lyric stopped right in front of him—if that wasn't just like a woman!—nearly causing them both to go down in a tangle as he grabbed her to keep from mowing her over.

"What?" she said, turning around and giving him a hostile glance from those big, brown eyes that could go incredibly soft—

Shaking off the fantasy, he said in a growl, "The rain is coming."

It hit them at that moment, a deluge of cold air and colder water, slanting across their faces, wrapping around their bodies like an icy blanket.

Her breasts beaded against her shirt…and against him. He felt them as two separate points of fire poking into his chest and reminding him of other times.

When he'd believed in her, he reminded himself ruthlessly. Before he'd known the *real* Lyric.

Stepping back, he urged her toward the house and, keeping a hand firmly against her back, propelled her across the yard and onto the porch. The wind snatched the screen door from his grasp and slammed it against the logs. Lyric got the heavy wooden door open, and the wind blew them inside. He managed to close both doors before they drowned.

"Look what the storm blew in," Uncle Nick said, relief in his smile. He stuck a match to the paper and kindling in the fireplace. A welcome blaze leaped over the logs.

"Lyric!" her aunt said. "Are you all right?"

"Yes. I'm sorry about making you worry. I, uh, got distracted and lost track of time."

"Trevor found you and now you're both home safely. That's the important thing."

Trevor noted the closeness of the two women as they exchanged hugs and felt a funny twinge in his chest. "We'd better get into something dry," he said gruffly.

"Yes," Lyric agreed, brushing at her aunt's blouse. "Look, I've gotten you wet, too."

Aunt Fay patted her niece's shoulder. "No matter. Go change, then we'll all sit in front of the fire and wait out the storm."

Trevor followed Lyric down the hall. In his room, he stripped his clothing, then waited to see if Lyric would use the shower. He heard the water come on at that moment.

His body reacted predictably to thoughts of her in the steamy cubicle, the water cascading over her smooth skin, the lather of a floral shampoo in her hair....

He cursed and paced the room. The wind hit the house like a thousand demons bent on revenge. Going to the window, he saw the rain was a mix of hail and sleet. If this kept up, the hay they hadn't yet cut would be flat on the ground. Did they have enough to make it through the winter?

He concentrated on this worry until the shower stopped. When he heard her door open and close, he pulled on a pair of sweatpants and crossed the hall.

As he'd expected, her aroma surrounded him, a caress of sweet scents that filled his head and made him dizzy. He tried a couple more curses, but they did no good. His body was stretched as tight as a violin string.

Foregoing hot water, he let the icy sluice from the deep mountain well pour over him until he was in danger of frostbite. Finally he adjusted the levers to warm water and quickly soaped and rinsed. After shaving, he returned to his room, debated about slacks and a white shirt, then snorted and pulled on the matching top to the gray sweats.

On second thought, he added a pair of briefs under the sweats…just in case his libido got out of control once more. That's all he needed—his pants looking like he'd erected a tent pole—

He opened his door at the same moment as Lyric. She stepped into the hall. Upon seeing him, she stopped, then nodded and continued down the hallway.

She wore a pink sweatsuit, except hers looked elegant compared to his old gray one. Pearl studs dotted her earlobes and a single baroque pearl dangled from a gold chain at her throat. No makeup, except for gloss on her lips. She looked good enough to eat.

His libido went on the alert. Thank heavens he'd put on the briefs. He smiled cynically.

"Travis called," his uncle said, looking up from the logs he was adding to the grate. He and the aunt were enjoying a cup of tea before the fire. "He wants to know if you two are going to brave the storm to come over for dinner. He and Alison will understand if you don't want to venture out again."

"I forgot about that." Trevor looked at Lyric, who was dressed for the occasion, he realized. She returned his gaze and waited for him to make the decision. He nodded. "We can take the truck."

The aunt glanced toward the windows where the hail tap-danced against the panes.

"It isn't far," he told her. "Their house is on the other side of that stand of firs across the road. We can drive almost to the front door."

"Good."

A wicked smile brightened Uncle Nick's face. "Mmm, I'll have you to myself all evening. Whatever shall we do to fill the hours?" He waggled his eyebrows at the aunt.

A tempest hit Trevor like the onslaught of the storm. If he and Lyric were in front of a crackling fire, safe from the weather and from intrusion, he knew what he would do.... He groaned silently.

"Monopoly is a good way to pass the time," Lyric said with a perfectly serious face.

Trevor rolled his eyes as the older folks laughed. "Here," he told Lyric, "wear this." He handed her a raincoat and grabbed a poncho for himself. "Ready?"

She kissed her aunt's cheek as if they would be gone for days instead of two or three hours, then went outside with him. Taking her elbow, they dashed to the pickup in a slight lull in the sleet and hail.

In less than a minute he braked to a stop beside the front steps of the other house on the ranch.

"I love big porches," Lyric said in admiring tones.

"Let's get out on your side. It's closest to the steps," he advised. "Ready? Set. Go."

She flung open the door and ran up the steps onto the covered porch in a flash. He did the same, giving the door a slam behind him. Driven by the wind, they arrived at the front door, breathless and laughing.

He didn't know what was funny, but he couldn't wipe the smile off his face. When she looked up at him, he was drawn into her dark honey gaze. Need and hunger forced him to grit his teeth, wiping out the unexpected merriment.

She went solemn, too.

Without thinking, he pushed a wayward lock of hair behind her ear. Her eyes searched his, probing into his soul and making him aware of how vulnerable he was to her...to this one woman out of all the hundreds he'd met during his lifetime. He bent his head.

The opening of the door saved him from making a fool of himself. "Come in," Travis invited.

Alison joined her husband. "Can you believe this weather? It's summer, for heaven's sake."

Trevor shook the moisture off his poncho and did

the same with Lyric's raincoat, then hung them on pegs in the entryway. "Hail knows no seasons in the mountains."

"Lyric, would you like a tour of the house?" Alison asked. "We still don't have furniture in some rooms, but you can see the layout."

Trevor followed his twin into the family room while the women took off on their inspection.

"Wine? Beer? Tea?" Travis stopped by a hostess cart. "Hot buttered rum?"

"I'll take the rum."

Travis filled two mugs with the hot drink. The men settled in leather chairs in front of the fire.

"So where did you find your guest?" his brother asked.

"Over near the line shack."

"Ah, yes."

Trevor inwardly winced at his twin's satisfied smile. He knew Travis and Alison sometimes made use of the line shack for a romantic tryst. The bunkbeds there weren't exactly comfortable, but sometimes a couple wasn't thinking strictly of comfort.

He groaned as his body reacted to the images that filled his head like the sugarplums of story and rhyme.

Laughter interrupted the visions. The two women returned. "Are you guys ready to go to the table?" his sister-in-law wanted to know.

"Sure," he said, rising. He realized he was hungry. It had been a long, hard day in more ways than one.

"Would you ladies like a glass of wine?" Travis asked, playing the host to perfection.

Trevor witnessed his twin's competence and the quiet happiness he saw in the blue eyes so like his own. The whole family had worried about Travis when Julie had died, but now things were good for him and Alison.

Trevor was glad for his brother and wished his own life was settled and serene. Last year he'd thought he'd found heaven in the heart of Texas. A joke, that. Ha-ha.

After the women had their wine, the foursome went to the dining room. The salads were already in place. Trevor sniffed the delectable aroma of roasting meat and vegetables. It whetted his appetite.

Among other things, he amended, glancing across the table where Travis seated Lyric. He did the same for his hostess.

Alison twinkled up at him. "Thank you, kind sir."

Blond-haired and green-eyed, she was a senator's daughter, at ease in any situation. She'd taken to ranch life like a hunting dog to water. Her sister, living on the next ranch over from them, had done the same.

Lyric, being raised on a ranch, was at home in the saddle. She knew about calving and getting the hay in the barn before a storm and all the other chores required of a rancher. She could ride and follow a trail—

He realized everyone was looking at him and that

he was the only one still standing. He quickly took his chair.

After the meal they played bridge in the family room. Alison was the most skillful at the game. Since Trevor was her partner, he was on the winning team, but Lyric and his twin gave them a challenge.

"You're good," Travis complimented his partner. "With a little practice, I believe we could whip up on them."

"Absolutely," Lyric agreed.

"No way." Alison hooked her arm through his. "Trev and I are unbeatable."

"Maybe," his twin said, "but only if he can keep his mind on the game."

Trevor managed a smile. It had been difficult to concentrate with Lyric seated to his right, her knee brushing his a couple of times as she sat forward in the excitement of the play.

Her cheeks wore a pretty flush, he noted. She'd enjoyed herself. At least one of them had. He managed a smile at his own fatalistic humor.

"I'll serve dessert," Alison told them after putting away the cards and score sheet. A distinct whimper came from the back of the house. "Oh-oh, a priority call. Logan is ready for his bottle."

"May I help?" Lyric asked.

"Sure."

The women went into the kitchen while he and Travis folded and stored the card table in the closet.

Travis added logs to the fire, and the men settled in their chairs with hot drinks again.

"Trav?"

"Yeah, bro?"

Trevor couldn't decide how to ask what he wanted to know. "How did you...when you met Alison, there were problems..."

"Are you referring to the past?"

His brother had lost his first wife in childbirth. Trevor was hesitant to discuss it. "Sort of. But not exactly. That is..."

"What is it you want to know?" Travis asked. "It's okay. I can talk about it now."

"It was hard for you to accept your feelings for Alison, right?"

Travis grimaced. "It was impossible at first." He spoke softly as he stared into the fire. "But there was the desire." He paused and glanced his way.

Trevor nodded. He couldn't deny that part.

"Then there were other things. The need to see her and be near her. The hunger to touch her. The longing... Like being turned inside out."

"Yeah."

"Is that the way you felt last fall when you came home from the rodeo circuit? You sort of turned inside yourself for a long time. That was after you met Lyric, wasn't it?"

Trevor sipped the hot rum mix while scenes of the endless winter ran through his mind. "She was engaged," he finally said. "I didn't know. Then I found out."

"Sometimes people mistake love for a friend for being in love," his twin suggested.

"He was in an accident. She stayed with him. She chose him…" He stopped. Some things were too painful to bring into the open. He would never forget that moment.

"She's here now, so she must have woke up to the truth. She came to you."

Trevor shook his head. "He died."

"From the accident?"

Trevor shrugged to indicate he didn't know. "Later. In March, I think. She said she hadn't been engaged since March. I'm not sure what happened between September and spring."

"If Lyric won't say, ask her aunt."

Pacing in front of the fire, Trevor frowned. "Uncle Nick, meddling old codger that he is, planned this whole thing." He waved his hand to encompass the whole impossible situation between him and Lyric. "Did he think I would take one look and fall at her feet?"

Okay, so his heart had felt as if it dropped off She-Devil peak when he'd realized she was in the car he'd run off the road. But that had been shock.

"It doesn't matter what he thinks," Travis murmured. "What do *you* think?"

Thankfully Trevor was spared the trouble of considering that question as the women returned. Lyric cuddled his nephew in her arms. The baby sucked busily on a bottle, his eyes locked on her face.

"Sit here," Travis said, getting to his feet and letting Lyric and the baby have the easy chair.

A knot of emotion rose from inside Trevor and lodged in his throat. With an effort, he tore his eyes from the homey little tableau and the tenderness in her face as she fed the baby: the glow in her eyes, the way the firelight played over her as she smiled...

There was something sad and hurting in the way she smiled. He wondered what she was thinking. Had the winter been as hard for her as it had been for him?

He swallowed the painful knot and kept his eyes fixated on the fire. Travis and Alison went to the kitchen to prepare dessert. He could hear their voices as if from far away. Only the suckling of the child and the crackle of the fire permeated the room he and Lyric and the baby occupied.

When Lyric put the baby to her shoulder, Trevor glanced their way. A mistake, that. Lyric was perfectly at ease with the youngster. She sang a nursery song as she patted his back. When he burped, she praised him and gave him the rest of the bottle. Logan smiled widely before settling back and finishing the milk. A minute later his eyes drooped sleepily and he let go the nipple.

"Is he done?" Alison asked softly, coming into the room.

"Yes." Lyric held up the bottle so she could see.

"Good. Let's put him to bed."

The two women left the room. A brightness, a gentleness, seemed to recede when they were gone.

Trevor released a deep breath, not realizing until that moment how tense he'd become while observing the Madonna and Child scene. That Lyric loved children and was used to them was obvious. He wondered where she'd gained her expertise.

Well, living on a ranch and all, a person handled a lot of babies, mostly of the nonhuman kind, but babies were babies. They required similar care. He had quite a bit of experience himself.

And he liked babies. All kinds. He liked the cycle of life and the bright aspect of a new generation. Each spring brought a renewal of hope. That was one reason he loved living on the ranch. It was the same for Lyric—

The painful knot formed again, just under his breastbone. It was better not to think of her and the thoughts they had shared last fall. In his heart spring had never arrived.

Alison and Lyric brought in thick slices of chocolate cake for each of them while Travis carried a tray with coffee. Trevor returned to his chair and accepted the plate Lyric handed him.

Her soft hair fell forward over her shoulder as she leaned down. He resisted an urge to smooth it back from her temples, to run his fingers through the fine silk as he had one brief period last fall and kiss her until they were dizzy with longing.

He sucked in a harsh breath and recalled that Uncle

Nick had always said it was better to suffer in silence than bemoan one's fate to the world. Stiff upper lip and all that.

Yeah.

Chapter Six

After a stormy weekend, the sky was clear and the sun hot on Monday. Sitting on the front porch, Lyric worked on the Sunday crossword puzzle while her aunt continued reading ranch magazines.

"Are you planning on taking up ranching again?" she asked the older woman after completing the last clue of the puzzle. Her aunt had sold her spread and moved to the city a couple of years after her father had established his law office in Austin. That was before he'd moved the family to his father's ranch outside of town.

Aunt Fay glanced up with a smile. "One never knows," she answered cheerfully.

Lyric studied her favorite relative. Her great-aunt

looked rested and happy. A startling idea came to Lyric—could there be something developing between her aunt and Trevor's uncle Nick?

Suddenly restless, Lyric stood. "I think I'll go for a ride if no one minds."

"Go on," her aunt urged. "Nick has to go to town. We're going to have lunch at their new lodge."

"It's a nice place. Mmm, I need to pick up my car today. Perhaps I should go with you."

"Trevor will take you this afternoon."

Lyric was a bit surprised at the quick suggestion, and a bit hurt. Her aunt preferred to be alone with Uncle Nick. She felt like the odd man out, the way she had at church yesterday when Jane Anne had sat by Trevor and claimed his attention before the service began. No one wanted her—

She broke the thought, forgoing self-pity and opting for fortitude. She only had two more weeks here at the Seven Devils Ranch. Anybody could last two weeks. She hoped. With a fatalistic sigh she let the restlessness claim her and rose from the comfortable chair.

Going to the paddock, she spotted Uncle Nick wrestling with a calf. "Let me help," she offered, entering a small pen and straddling the struggling calf. She held it in place while he treated a sore on its neck. After lancing the spot, he cleaned it, then applied an antibiotic cream.

"That'll do," he said. They returned the calf to the herd. It ran bawling to its mother. "Thanks for your help. You know your way around a ranch,'' the older man said.

"I've lived on one since I was nearly ten."

"How old are you now?"

"Twenty-four."

"Trevor is twenty-eight. He's the last of the orphans," he said, his manner introspective as they leaned on the railing and watched the cattle in the pasture.

"The last to marry," she murmured and thought of his neighbor. Jane Anne was eighteen, maybe nineteen. Young, but used to ranch life, too.

"My boys are all honorable men," the uncle continued.

Lyric nodded. She hadn't met the girl cousin or the doctor or the cousin who was an attorney, but Trevor, Travis and Zack were poured from the same mold. Like their uncle, they were men of the land, steadfast and capable.

"If you seduced him—"

The earth gave a gigantic lurch under Lyric's feet.

"—he would marry you, so don't worry about that."

She shook her head even as hope flared like a new star in her. Trevor had made his feelings clear on that issue.

Tell him you already tried that and it didn't work, he'd said, furious that he'd given in to the tumultuous, irresistible passion.

"He thinks I'm a liar and a cheat," she said with total honesty. She even managed a smile.

The keen Dalton eyes met hers. "Are you?"

"I…I don't know. When we met last year, I was supposed to be considering my feelings toward someone else, an old friend who thought we should marry, but I wasn't sure how I felt. Then Trevor visited my aunt and we met. It was… There was an attraction. It made everything confusing."

"Do you know how you feel now?"

"Yes," she said. "More confused."

The old uncle smiled with her as she adopted a light tone for her admission. "Don't worry about it," he advised. "There's plenty of time. You and your aunt don't really have to return to Texas at the end of the month, do you?"

Trevor had been silent on the trip back to the main house after dinner with his twin and Alison Saturday night. He'd hardly looked her way, much less spoken since then. If only she'd told him the truth from the first, perhaps things would have been different for them. But she hadn't and he hated her for the deception. Rightfully.

For every act there was a consequence…

"We have to go," she said, squashing the desperate longing that made her want to agree to stay.

"Mmm," he said as if he didn't quite believe her, but he dropped the subject. "Are you going for a ride? Sal is restless. I think she expects you."

Lyric nodded. She had a plan.

* * *

The line shack was where Uncle Nick had said it was supposed to be, Lyric discovered that afternoon. She had ridden out immediately after lunch while the older couple settled down for their naps, her aunt on the sofa, the uncle in the leather recliner.

Travis and Trevor were back in the alfalfa fields. Alison was at her house tending to the baby. Lyric felt free to do whatever she wished, which was look for the little girl who'd lost her barrette.

The cabin, with its wooden sides weathered to silver, was almost invisible against the trees growing up the slope behind it. After inspecting the area, Lyric knew the poachers hadn't been using it.

Reining the mare westward, she rode across the meadow. The carcass had been reduced to a loose collection of bones. Chipmunks and voles would gnaw on them for the minerals during the coming months.

Without pausing, she headed for the woodland trail and followed it to a ridge that opened onto a wonderful view of a narrow valley and the seven peaks that lined the Snake River. A haze hung over the trees, and the breeze carried a hint of wood smoke.

She glanced back along the trail, then turned determinedly to face the wind. She would follow the scent to its source, if possible.

An hour later, her hunch paid off when she came upon a campsite tucked neatly into a wooded cove with a rocky overhang sheltering it somewhat from the wind. A large tent was set up among the trees. A fire pit held the hot embers of burnt logs. Thin strips of meat dried on a wooden frame over the fire. Not a soul was about.

The hair stood up on Lyric's neck.

She tied Sal to a shrub and quietly scouted the outer boundaries of the camp. Damp clothing hung over a line stretched between two trees. A basin had been dug and lined with stones to catch the trickle of water from a tiny creek.

After a searching sweep of the area, Lyric went into the camp and studied the footprints between the fire pit and the tent. She recognized the girl's among the three sets of prints. This indeed was the poachers' camp.

But where were they?

Perhaps she was being foolish, but Lyric felt no fear of this little group. There were no signs of liquor or riotous living. The campsite was one of neat efficiency.

The tent, when she peered cautiously inside, was the same. Three sleeping bags were lined up side by side, a duffel bag at the end of each. She refrained from searching those, feeling that was too much of an intrusion.

After considering the time, she waited an hour for someone to return. No one showed up.

Finally, reluctantly, she took the mare to the creek and let her drink her fill, then mounted up. It would be after six before she got back to the ranch house, but she'd warned her aunt and Trevor's uncle that she planned to be out all afternoon. She certainly didn't want anyone searching for her again.

Two hours later, safely home, she unsaddled and brushed the mare, then put her out to pasture. Trevor was feeding several animals located in pens next to the paddock. She hesitated as her heart skipped a couple of beats, then she went over to him.

"Orphans?" she asked, stopping at the gate to one pen that held three calves.

"Yeah. These came from one mother. She didn't make it through the birthing." He set two pails of formula in front of two calves and held a third one for the smallest of the bunch.

"Triplets. That's rather unusual."

He nodded.

"They look like Black Angus, except they're red."

"About one in a hundred are. I've never seen three reds born at the same time, though."

"Strange things can happen," she said lightly. "Perhaps it was the phase of the moon."

He cut her a hard glance. "Yeah."

Her mood darkened at his tone. "Like when we met," she continued softly. "We both were obviously under a delusion."

"What the hell does that mean?"

"We each thought the other was something else."

Before she could leave, he muttered, "Right. I thought you were a walking dream, but I found I was having a nightmare instead."

"So was I," she told him.

"I never lied to *you*."

"I didn't lie to you, either."

"You just failed to mention you were engaged to another man," he accused, moving the bucket and earning a reprimand from the hungry calf.

"I've explained all that to you. Yes, I should have told you the situation, but things moved too fast. I was confused by what was happening between us. I'd never felt that way before. Then, when I realized how serious it was, I knew I had to tell you about Lyle, but there was never a good time."

"In three weeks, you couldn't find an opportunity to mention you were promised to another man?" he demanded. "Like, 'By the way I just happen to be engaged'? You couldn't have said that?"

She shook her head.

He snorted and stalked into the barn to prepare feed for the other orphans in the pens. Lyric headed for the house to bathe and change for dinner. It wasn't until she was in the shower that she remembered she'd been going to tell him about the camp hidden in the woods.

Trevor ignored the fresh scent of Lyric's soap and cologne while he showered. Tired and out of sorts, he washed quickly, dried and dressed in fresh jeans and shirt. He went to the dining room in his socks.

Lyric and her aunt both looked up when he entered.

The aunt smiled. Lyric didn't. They finished placing the food on the table. "It's ready," Aunt Fay said.

"Where's Uncle Nick?" he asked.

"Right here."

The older man appeared, freshly bathed and shaved and dressed in dark slacks and a white shirt. He'd checked and treated the cattle for pink eye and other maladies most of the day, putting in a full day's work, just as Trevor and Travis had. A surge of affection filled Trevor. If he were half the man his uncle was, he'd count himself a success in life.

"Allow me," his uncle said, and, with a show of gallantry, seated Lyric's aunt.

Trevor realized he could do no less. He held Lyric's chair for her, but stopped short of snapping her napkin open and placing it in her lap as his uncle had done with the older woman. He nodded at Lyric's murmured Thank you.

"You had a long ride this afternoon," he now said to her. "I'd thought we would go into town and pick up your car. It's ready."

"I forgot about it," she said, looking contrite. "Out here, I haven't needed it."

"It's nice to meet a woman who's content to be in the country instead of wanting to run to town every minute," Uncle Nick said with a warm smile in Lyric's direction, then a stern glance in his.

Trevor didn't need the message written out. His uncle thought Lyric would make the perfect ranch wife.

"So," he said, deliberately sardonic, "did you track the poachers down this afternoon?"

She didn't look his way, but instead spoke to the older man. "Sort of. I found their camp."

He sat up straight. "What?"

"The three have a camp over the next ridge, about an hour from the line shack. They're drying the meat over a fire pit. There's a tent, too, and—"

"You went into their camp?" he demanded, so furious he wanted to shake some sense into her.

She flashed him one of her mulish looks. "No one was there, but I found the same sets of prints."

Trevor groaned and controlled the fury with an effort. "I can't believe you were so stupid—"

"It wasn't stupid. I circled the camp first and made sure it was empty. It was. Then I checked it out."

"They could have been waiting in the woods to ambush you."

"I made it back okay, didn't I?" she reminded him, her tone as cutting as his.

Trevor glared. She glared back.

Her true colors had emerged over the past week. Gone was the sweet, ardent woman he'd found in Texas. In her place was this stubborn female who thought she could handle any situation, who ignored his warnings and him, most of the time.

"I called Zack after I got back to the house," she now said to the others.

"What for?" he wanted to know.

"Since he's a deputy sheriff, I thought it was *his* business to know about the poachers."

Trevor nodded stiffly.

"He's coming out in the morning. We're going over to the camp—"

"Zack and I'll go," Trevor interrupted. "You'll stay here at the house."

"I'm the one who found the place."

"You can give us directions."

"I'm going, too."

Trevor became aware of their relatives observing the argument with great interest…and amusement, although they were trying to hide it. Heat flowed up his neck and into his ears. He shrugged.

"Zack will be here at first light. We plan to be at the camp before six and maybe catch them sleeping," she told the other two as if there'd been no break in the conversation.

"Good," Uncle Nick said.

"I know you'll be careful," the aunt told Lyric.

"Of course."

She glanced at him as if expecting another argument, but he kept his mouth shut. He'd just make sure she stayed behind him and out of the way in case of trouble. A sigh worked its way out. Life had seemed simple once.

"Let's play some cards after supper," his uncle suggested. "I believe the wisdom of age can whip the socks off the rashness of youth."

"Very funny," Trevor muttered, grinning in spite of his irritation with Lyric.

They played an old card game called Rook. The seniors did win, but it was a close call, decided on the last hand.

Oddly, when Trevor went to bed, he felt good. It had been a fun evening. He and Lyric had played to each other's strengths, as if they'd been partners in some other lifetime and knew each other's minds.

In bed with the light out and the sheet drawn up to ward off the coolness of the night, his mind roamed at will, lingering on the winter just past, then zeroing in on the autumn. If there'd been no old boyfriend in the background, would he and Lyric have been married by now?

Would it have been a mistake?

She'd stuck by her lifelong friend when the man had been ill, ill enough to die. If there'd been no accident, would she have chosen him over the other?

Okay, so he hadn't understood the seriousness of the situation when he'd left Texas. He'd thought she'd rejected him, but maybe…maybe she hadn't wanted to. Her mother had put a lot of pressure on her. Living with Uncle Nick, he knew what that was like.

The timing between them may have been off, but the passion had been real. She'd responded as wildly to their kisses as he had…last fall and last week.

She hadn't faked her response to him. It may have been induced by grief, but it had been real.

He shifted restlessly as his blood warmed at the memory of their lovemaking. Like his twin had said—there was the passion, but there was also the need to be with her, to explore the world through her eyes.

Was that love?

Uncle Nick said he would know when it came along. Last year he would have agreed, now...he didn't know what his feelings were. Or hers, truth to tell. At any rate he wasn't going to rush into anything again, all moony-eyed and thinking he was in love. He'd learned that much.

Satisfied that this was the wise thing to do, he closed his eyes and willed sleep to come.

Lyric heard the sheriff's cruiser before it swept under the huge log at the entrance to the ranch compound. She finished buttoning her shirt and pulled on a pair of boots.

There, she was ready for the excursion to capture the poachers. She wanted to be there because she thought the lawmen might be surprised at what they found.

Going to the kitchen, she found Trevor and his uncle there. Bacon and eggs were ready. Uncle Nick removed a pan of biscuits from the oven. "You'll need a hot meal before you leave," he told her. "It could be a long day."

Zack, the twins' older brother, joined them. "The

sheriff said for me to deputize you and Travis. He's going with us.''

Trevor nodded.

A minute later the other twin entered the main ranch house. Like Trevor, he was dressed in jeans, a long-sleeved work shirt and boots. Gloves were tucked into his back pocket. He tossed a hat on the rack by the front door and joined them.

"It's going to be hot today," he said. "The temperature is already in the fifties."

"What's the plan?" Uncle Nick asked, looking at Zack.

The deputy washed down a bite of egg with milk. "We'll circle around and come in from the west side. If they run, we'll herd them toward the line shack or the house here."

The uncle nodded. "I'll be ready."

Lyric spared a worry for her aunt. "There won't be trouble," she said. "They only have one gun."

"Sometimes people panic," Zack warned her. "You're to stay with Trevor and do exactly what he says."

When she glanced at Trevor, he met her eyes levelly and with a seriousness that stopped any protest. She knew the three brothers would protect her with their lives. "I won't get in the way," she promised.

The men nodded, taking her word for her good behavior.

Zack glanced at his watch, then the window. "Let's go. I want to catch them asleep."

"Are we going in trucks?" Travis asked. "We can make it across the upper meadow, but then we'll have to walk."

"Horses," the deputy said. "We'll take two extra mounts to bring them in. The girl can ride with one of us."

The planning session was short and to the point, Lyric observed. From a lifetime of working together, each brother knew what to expect of the other.

She suddenly missed her two younger siblings. Both had taken jobs in the oil fields that summer, living at the drilling site in a used trailer and sharing an adventure. Like the Daltons, the three of them had worked together on their ranch, too. Until their parents' divorce, she'd thought they were a happy family.

She still didn't understand how they could throw out all those years of marriage. Glancing at Trevor, she decided he was right to be wary of involvement. Although her grandparents had been married for over sixty years, love didn't seem to last in modern times.

"Let's go," Zack said, rising.

She saw everyone had finished the meal except her. She downed the last bite of biscuit and egg, then stood. At the paddock, they saddled up four mounts for them and two for the poachers. She wasn't surprised when the men strapped pistols around their hips and rifles to their saddles.

An hour later they headed down the slope and across the meadow in a direct line from the emergency cabin. From there they followed the game trail to the ridge. Zack motioned for them to dismount.

They quietly guided the horses to a tiny glen beside a seasonal creek, dry now except for a few pools in shady spots. She hadn't known it was there. After tying the horses to saplings, the men retrieved their rifles.

Gazing at the mountains, which were just becoming visible in the early-morning haze, she realized the Daltons knew this land as well as they knew the layout of their homes. When she'd described the camping area, they'd known where it was immediately.

Realizing they'd let her accompany them rather than argue about it, she followed behind as Trevor circled one side of the camp and his brothers circled the other. A short time later, she heard the call of an owl.

Trevor cupped his hands around his mouth and answered in the same pattern. They were ready.

The fresh scent of smoke wafted around her, faint at first, then stronger. She glanced at Trevor to see if he caught it, too. He nodded. Motioning for her to follow, he handed her the pistol and positioned the rifle at his side.

A shrill whistle rent the air.

Trevor rushed forward. From the opposite side of the camp, Zack and Travis burst from the woods, weapons ready.

"Police! Don't move!" the deputy ordered the boy who was adding wood chips to the fire pit.

He froze. Fear flashed over his face, then was gone. "Run!" he shouted.

The tent flap was pushed aside and the young girl appeared.

Behind her, Lyric sensed movement before she heard the click of a gun being cocked.

"Drop your guns," said a deeper male voice, "or the woman gets it."

Snapping her head around, she met the unfriendly gaze of the young man who spoke. He was the oldest of the three culprits and looked to be around eighteen.

"It's okay," she said, instinctively knowing the youngsters needed help. She walked toward him.

"Don't come any closer," he ordered. His tone was rough, threatening.

She kept moving slowly. "We're here to help."

"Right," he said, aiming the high-powered rifle at a point in the middle of her forehead. At this distance he wouldn't miss.

Lyric took another step. She heard Trevor curse softly, then his steps behind her. "Don't," she said, casting a glance over her shoulder. She faced the teenager, saw the desperation in his eyes.

"I don't want to hurt you," he warned.

"No one is going to get hurt," she told him, holding his stare. "No one."

She laid her hand on the barrel of the gun and smiled gently at the youth who was trying so hard to protect his little clan.

Chapter Seven

Trevor tightened his hold on Lyric's shoulder, gauging his chances of thrusting her aside before the boy could pull the trigger. It was the only chance he had of saving her, and he figured he'd only get one go at it.

"We can help you," Lyric promised, her tone gentle, her body resistant to any pressure from him to move aside. She'd apparently forgotten about the pistol he'd given her. It was pointed at a spot beside her foot.

Damn stubborn woman.

For a second, despair seized him the way it had when, as a boy, he'd realized that being trapped in an avalanche meant his parents were never coming home. He tensed, ready to spring on the gunman—

The rifle barrel wavered, then dropped until it pointed at the ground. Trevor rushed in before the youth could change his mind. Wrenching the rifle away with one hand, he shoved his own rifle under his arm, caught the culprit's arm and, using the thumb for leverage, brought it up behind his back, forcing him to bend forward, rendering him harmless.

"Trevor, don't," Lyric implored in the same soft voice. "Don't hurt him. He was protecting his family."

She touched his arm, her doe-soft eyes pleading for the youth. Trevor, against his better judgment, loosened his hold marginally.

Zack came over and snapped handcuffs on the young man, who was giving them a defiant scrutiny laced with fury.

"They're not going to Family Services," the boy said, his eyes darting to the other two youngsters, then back to Zack. "I can take care of them."

"By teaching them to steal?" Trevor asked, still itching to pound the younger man for endangering a woman. He tried to calm the adrenaline-induced anger when Lyric flicked him an anxious glance.

"We'll talk about it," his brother promised. "When we get to the ranch."

"What ranch?" the culprit demanded as if he had a right to information.

"Seven Devils. You're in the national forest. Our land starts at the top of the ridge. The meadow where you poached the calf belongs to us,'' Trevor told him. "Also the calf.''

The youth shrugged. "We needed the meat.''

"Is this all the gear you have?'' Zack asked, peering into the tent.

"It's everything we own in the world. The law has taken everything else from us. You going to take that, too?''

For sheer bravado, Trevor had to admire the youth and his little band of thieves. The three stood steadfast and defiant around the fire pit while the two Dalton brothers checked out the camp and Trevor stood guard.

Zack got out his notebook and pen when he finished the quick search. "Names?'' he said. "And ages.''

This was greeted with stony silence.

"Can't we question them at the house?'' Lyric asked. "Maybe after they eat lunch.''

Trevor snorted. Women always thought food would help a situation. He waited for Zack to make the decision.

His older brother nodded. "Let's break camp and get on the way. I need to get back to the office sometime today.''

After storing the tent and utensils in a backpack hanging from a rope behind the tent, then burying the strips of meat and smothering the fire, the lawmen were ready to take their prisoners to the ranch house.

Lyric, he noted, cast a worried glance at the three-some, then at Zack, as they loaded up the horses.

"Okay if the girl rides with you?" Zack asked her.

"Of course."

His brother hoisted the girl onto Lyric's horse in front of her. "It's okay," he heard Lyric murmur to the child, who was silent with the stoicism of some-one who was used to life's uncertainties. The two boys were mounted on the spare horses along with their gear. Zack held the older one's reins while Travis took the other.

Trevor brought up the rear of the group. He would keep on eye on the odd little bunch of thieves just to be sure they didn't try anything. Two hours later they arrived at the house. Uncle Nick and Lyric's aunt came out on the porch and waited for the group to dismount.

"These are the poachers?" Uncle Nick asked when the three were herded onto the porch.

"Yes," Zack said. "We caught them red-handed, you might say. They were drying meat over a fire."

"That was to get us through the winter. You wouldn't have missed one calf," the older of the culprits lashed out at them.

"Cattle are our livelihood," Uncle Nick said with-out rancor. "That's what gets us through the winter, too." He held the door open. "Let's go inside and try to get to the bottom of this."

"We need to wash up," Lyric told the men, indi-cating the girl and herself.

"Good idea. Show 'em the way." Uncle Nick checked the time. "We'll eat, then talk."

Zack, officially in charge of the investigation, didn't argue, Trevor noticed. Not that it would have done any good. When their uncle gave an order, people listened.

While Lyric took the girl down the hall to that bathroom, Zack herded the two boys along the east wing to another. He let them go in one at a time. This ensured they didn't try anything while inside, such as climbing out the window and escaping.

Trevor thought the youth who'd appointed himself guardian of the other two would be reluctant to leave the girl in any case. The boy was protective.

When they returned, Uncle Nick, who'd become a mother hen in his old age, urged everyone to the table. A platter of scrambled eggs and bacon awaited them, along with biscuits, cinnamon rolls and mugs of hot chocolate for the two younger guests. There was coffee for the adults, including the oldest of the poachers.

Lyric seated the girl between herself and her aunt. The two boys sat on Uncle Nick's left along with his brothers. Trevor took a place at the end of the table opposite his uncle. Lyric was on his right.

To an outsider, it must have appeared very peaceful and family oriented, but all present were aware of the tension.

The younger kids looked to the older one before accepting food. He hesitated, then nodded. The girl and boy ate rapidly, but with good manners. Their protector did the same after a frown around the table as if to say sharing a meal wasn't going to soften him up.

"The weatherman says it'll be clear the rest of the week, so we can finish the alfalfa field," Uncle Nick commented. He and the aunt drank coffee while the others ate.

Trevor, like his brothers, was also hungry. The five-hour round trip had used up the very early breakfast they'd all had. Lyric, too, was working on a full plate.

She glanced up and caught his eyes on her. An unexpected smile lit her face for a second before she asked the child at her side about having seconds. He realized she was relieved and happy at finding the little group of poachers, especially the girl, who didn't look more than ten, as Lyric had estimated. The boy was maybe thirteen while their guardian was around eighteen.

Okay, so she'd been right about the thieves. They were kids. Runaways? His gut instinct said they were. But from what—family, the law, or the welfare service the older boy had mentioned? His gaze met Zack's. It was time to find out.

"Trevor, you want to pour us another cup of coffee?" Uncle Nick requested.

"Sure."

"Would you like another cup of hot chocolate?" Lyric asked the two kids.

After a glance at the older boy, they nodded.

Trevor allowed her to precede him into the kitchen.

He got out the cocoa mix while she put milk into the children's mugs. He refreshed the coffee cups in the dining room and returned to the kitchen.

"What do you think about them?" she asked in a near whisper while they waited for the milk mixture to heat in the microwave.

"Runaways," he said.

She nodded. "They're orphans."

"How do you know?"

"The oldest mentioned Family Services."

"Maybe they were taken from their home."

"Maybe." She looked doubtful. "But they have good manners. They respect authority, too."

"What makes you think that?"

"They defer to the older boy."

"They don't have much respect for the law. Killing other people's cattle is a serious offense."

She nodded. "Survival takes precedence, though. They did what they felt they had to do."

"The way you did with your fiancé?" He wished he hadn't said that, but the words were out before he could stop them.

The soft-as-velvet eyes met his squarely. "That was a matter of honor. Would you have run out on a dying friend?"

She removed the two mugs when the microwave beeped and returned to the table, leaving him frowning and trying to think of something to say that wouldn't make him look like a heel. Nothing came to mind.

* * *

Lyric took her seat and touched the young girl's arm reassuringly when Zack once more pulled out his notebook and pen. His manner suggested he wasn't in the mood for nonsense from the three poachers.

"Names," he said, glancing at the oldest. "I'll start with you."

After a brief internal struggle, the guardian answered, "Jeremy Aquilon. This one is my...cousin, Antonio."

Lyric wondered if the hesitation meant Jeremy was lying or had considered lying but decided on the truth. She couldn't tell.

"This is Krista, also my cousin and Antonio's sister."

"Address?" Zack asked.

Jeremy shrugged, a cynical half smile on his lips. "The forest. Nowhere," he added at a sharp frown from the deputy.

The lawman was apparently used to such answers. He continued. "What was your last-known address?"

"A rented trailer in Boise. Lucky Peak RV Park."

"Mother died," the girl, Krista, interjected.

Jeremy gave her a warning glance, then his chest lifted and dropped in a silent sigh. "My aunt got in front of a stray bullet during a shoot-out between two neighbors over a card game. She died."

Zack nodded. "What about your parents?"

Jeremy shrugged. "My mother ran out long ago.

My father died of a heart attack at thirty-nine. My aunt took me in when I was twelve.''

"Is there an uncle to go with the aunt?"

"There was. My dad's brother. He and my aunt were divorced. He rolled his truck and died six months before my father's death of a heart attack. We don't have any grandparents still living.''

Zack turned to the younger orphans. "How old are you, Krista?''

She ducked her head and didn't answer.

"She's ten. Tony is thirteen. I'm eighteen, old enough to care for them,'' Jeremy stated, his eyes defiant and older than his years.

So were Tony's and Krista's, Lyric thought, much too old for their ages.

"But you weren't last year,'' Trevor said. "You headed for the hills last summer. Why?''

The muscles stood out in Jeremy's jaw as his lips thinned in fury, but he didn't reply.

"We were put in a foster home,'' Antonio finally told them, his eyes downcast. "Krista and I were. I ran away and found Jeremy.''

"Trouble?'' Zack asked, his tone gentle.

"The man,'' Antonio said in a near whisper. "The man beat us. He whipped Krista for dropping a plate, so hard her legs bled.'' The boy looked at his sister, then down at his hands again. "Jeremy took us away that night.''

Lyric experienced a rush of anger so strong it was all she could do to stay in her seat. She looked at

Trevor and saw the same barely controlled fury. He shook his head slightly, telling her to keep quiet.

"So you came up here," Zack concluded. "Where did you live during the winter?"

Jeremy nodded his head toward the east. "There's an abandoned gas station in town. It has an apartment upstairs."

Travis spoke up. "Shelby looked at the place. It was uninhabitable, so Beau let her have his cabin on the lake."

Shelby was Beau's nurse, Lyric recalled. And his wife.

Zack frowned. "You stayed there undetected? How did you cook or stay warm?"

"There was a kerosene heater. The place was drafty enough that we didn't have to worry about fumes," Jeremy explained with a shrug. "I stocked groceries at night at the market. I told the manager I was new in town and that my dad was out of a job. He let me have damaged fruit and vegetables, also cans without labels."

"We made soup. It was fun." Krista put a hand over her mouth and looked at her cousin as if wondering if she'd said too much.

Jeremy smiled at the girl. "It was," he agreed. "We never knew until we opened a can what we were going to make for dinner."

Lyric's heart melted right down to her toes at the young man's gentleness with his cousin. Whatever it took, she was going to help them stay together and away from foster parents who were supposed to protect children, not take their frustrations out on them.

"Okay, I get the picture," Zack said, flipping the notebook closed. "I'll have to call the office and see what's to be done next."

Jeremy clenched his hands into fists. "Tony and Krista stay with me."

"That's for the court to decide," Zack said, again in a gentle manner.

The muscles of Jeremy's jaw flexed again. The other two looked frightened.

"Perhaps," Lyric said slowly, thinking it through as she spoke, "perhaps they could stay with me until…until we get some legal advice."

The uncle nodded. "We'll have Seth look into it. He's a lawyer. He'll know what to do."

Jeremy shook his head. "You don't know Family Services," he said bitterly. "My uncle took me in and agreed to take them, too, but the case worker said he wasn't blood kin to Tony and Krista and his place wasn't approved as a foster home, so they were taken away. That's what the law does to people."

"If they aren't blood kin, then how come they have the same last name?" Zack asked.

The young man took a slow, careful breath while he considered his answer. "Their mom was married to someone else before my uncle, but they've always used the same name. I think my uncle adopted them."

Something more to be checked out, Lyric realized. "If we provide a stable home," she began, then stopped. "I'm not a resident here, though. I'll have to find a place—"

"Then you would have to get it approved," Jeremy told her. "You think that can be done in less than a year? Besides, you're not married, are you?"

"No, but—"

"Then forget it," he advised. "The court wants foster kids to have a family environment."

He was so cynical it hurt Lyric deep inside. An eighteen-year-old shouldn't have to lose his faith in justice. She turned to her aunt. "We can help, can't we?"

"We'll certainly try," Aunt Fay said, her eyes gleaming with determination.

The older woman could be as stubborn as her niece at times. Lyric relaxed. She had a friend on her side.

"We won't put up with any nonsense from the welfare people," Uncle Nick chimed in. "You three will stay here until *I'm* satisfied you have a safe place."

Lyric settled back into her chair. "How do I get in touch with the attorney you mentioned? Seth, as in Dalton, right?"

"Yes," Trevor said. "He's our cousin. We'll go to town and see him."

"And pick up my car. Aunt Fay and I need to look for a place to rent until this is straightened out."

"This is where you'll all stay until we get this settled," the Dalton uncle declared. "No judge will say this ranch isn't a safe place for children. Besides, it was approved when my nephews and niece came to live with me.''

A triumphant gleam in his Dalton-blue eyes, he grinned at Lyric. She grinned back. Now that she had a fighting team assembled, she felt much better. ''All will be well,'' she assured the three orphans.

Seth Dalton was a complete surprise to Lyric when she and Trevor arrived for their ten-o'clock appointment the next morning. He looked like a pirate with his swarthy skin and, most surprising of all, dark, dark eyes. The Dalton blue-eyed gene had skipped him altogether. He was a bit shorter than Trevor, with muscular shoulders that were evident under his conservative suit and white shirt.

''Trev, old man, how are you?'' he greeted them when they were shown into his office. ''You must be Lyric.''

''Yes. Thank you for seeing us on such short notice,'' she said.

He shook her hand, then held it as he guided her to a chair and saw that she was comfortably seated. ''Coffee? Tea? Something to eat?''

''Uh, no, thank you.''

''Oh, Amelia wants you two to come over for lunch when we're done here. Can you make it?''

''Yes,'' Trevor answered for them. ''Got any of Amelia's scones here?''

''Sorry, they're gone.''

"My car," Lyric reminded Trevor firmly, feeling rather adrift as the conversation flowed around her.

"We'll pick it up after lunch." Trevor turned to his cousin. "Did you get the information you needed from Zack and Uncle Nick?"

"Yes." Seth looked at an open folder on his desk. "I've taken the liberty of talking to the county judge. He's put the Aquilon kids in Uncle Nick's custody for the time being. His office will call the juvenile judge in Boise and request jurisdiction be moved up here."

"Man, you work fast," Trevor said in admiration.

Seth gave them a satisfied smile, looking so much like a swashbuckler, Lyric wouldn't have been surprised if he'd pulled out a sword and waved it over his head. Like the other Daltons she knew, he was a force to be reckoned with.

And another plus for her side. "I, uh, thought I would ask for custody. I head up a foundation that sometimes takes an interest in cases like this."

"You wouldn't happen to be a social worker, would you?"

She hesitated, then said, "Not exactly. I have a degree in sociology as well as business. I've done…that is, the foundation has sponsored in-depth reports on special cases at times."

"How about checking out the uncle Jeremy mentioned? If we showed the court the kids would be safe there, I think that would be the best place for them.

They need family around them. You two could go down to Boise tomorrow—''

''Wait a minute,'' Trevor interrupted his cousin's planning. ''Trav and I are in the middle of cutting hay.''

''I can fill in for you on Saturday. Uncle Nick said he would drive the tractor. Beau says it's okay.''

Lyric tried to sort the names out. Beau was the doctor. He thought it was okay for their uncle to cut hay. Beau and Seth were brothers and they had a younger sister. With Zack, Trevor and Travis, there were six Daltons.

And Uncle Nick. That made seven. Seven Daltons. Seven Devils Mountains. Mmm…

She wiped the smile off her face when she realized the other two were looking at her. ''Sorry, what did you say?''

''I asked if you were willing to stay and see this through. There may be legal expenses if we have to use an attorney in Boise.''

''Of course I'll stay. The foundation has a special fund we can draw on. My father is on the board of directors. I'll have to get an okay from him, but I don't see a problem.''

''Good. Be sure you get statements from neighbors on this uncle. I need to present it to the judge. The court date is next week.''

''Next week!'' Lyric and Trevor said in unison.

Seth grinned. ''Yeah. I believe in moving fast. Besides, they had an opening.'' He glanced at the clock on the mantel. "Time for my next appointment. I'll see you two at the B and B in thirty minutes."

"B and B?" Lyric asked when she and Trevor were outside the large Victorian house that had been converted to a doctor's office for Beau and an attorney's office for Seth.

"Seth's wife runs a bed and breakfast here in town. Zack's wife, Honey, has a dance studio in the old carriage house there. You'll probably meet her, too."

"Talk about family togetherness," Lyric murmured once they were in the truck and on the way. "Seth and Beau have offices together. Two of the wives have businesses in the same location."

"My cousin Roni is married to Honey's brother."

Trevor grinned when Lyric groaned. "I'm never going to keep this straight," she told him.

"Don't worry about it," he advised.

Because she was only there for a visit and would soon be gone. Because she wasn't part of the Dalton family and wasn't going to be.

To her horror, hot tears rushed to her eyes. They filled her throat so she couldn't speak for a second. She held on desperately and slowly conquered the misery. By the time they stopped on an apron of gravel in front of another Victorian home on a side street of the town, she was in control once more.

"This is lovely," she murmured as they mounted the broad steps to the leaded glass front door.

Before they could ring the bell, the door opened. "Come in. I've been waiting for you. I want to hear all about the poachers you caught. You must be Lyric. I'm Amelia. I'm so glad to meet you. Uncle Nick called Seth and told us all about you and your aunt last night.''

Lyric was swept into a great room that smelled of cinnamon and cloves and flowers.

"Come to the sitting room. We'll have an iced-tea cooler while we wait for Seth,'' Amelia continued.

The private sitting room was at the back of the house. From its windows, Lyric stared at the backyard, a riot of flowers and vegetables, and beyond to the mountains, rising like guardians on the horizon.

"This is so lovely,'' Lyric told the other woman. "The flowers. And the view. Your home is so welcoming.''

Amelia was as lovely as…not a rose, not with that curly auburn hair, cool-blue eyes and heart-shaped face.

Lyric's gaze rested on a tall, regal canna lily in the garden. It was brilliant red with a golden throat. That was it. Amelia had the warmth and beauty of the lily.

"Thank you. Please be seated. I'll be right back.''

After their hostess left the room, Lyric glanced at the sofa, then chose a rocking chair in colorful chintz. A cat appeared and hopped into her lap, its motor already running in a happy purr.

"Hi, little one,'' Lyric said, rubbing the soft black-and-white ball of fur.

Trevor stood at one of the windows, his forehead

furrowed as if he were lost in deep, dark thoughts. She had an inkling of what they were.

"I can make the trip to Boise by myself," she told him. "I don't need anyone to help me with the report. I've done this kind of thing lots of times."

"You don't know the city. I do. It'll be quicker if we work together." He flashed her a sardonic glance. "I'll drive. You direct."

"Aunt Fay can go," she said stubbornly.

"It will probably be a long day before we get back to the ranch. Uncle Nick would worry about her."

"Oh."

He sat in one of the easy chairs that formed a conversational grouping around a fireplace. "They have a thing going. Haven't you noticed?"

It had occurred to her, but only briefly. His comment brought the situation home to her.

He shrugged at her troubled glance.

"She's sixty-eight. He's...?"

"Seventy-one." His smile was mocking. "Age doesn't matter. Love knows no boundaries."

"I can see you know all about it," she murmured a bit waspishly.

His glance flicked to her, then to the window once more. "No," he said, becoming serious. "Not me. I don't know anything."

She knew he was thinking of them and all that had happened. If she'd loved him, as she'd indicated in her letter, then why hadn't she come to him? She could sense the question inside him, tormenting him with what might have been, the way it tormented her.

Why hadn't she followed him once it was clear Lyle had survived the accident? Why had a sense of loyalty to her old friend taken precedence over her feelings for Trevor?

Her mother and Lyle's had convinced her that her place was at his side. It was her duty to make his last days happy ones. She'd done her best but…but she'd lost something in the ordeal. Not just Trevor and a chance for their love, but a part of herself…

Again she felt the terrible struggle inside herself that had raged while she sat beside Lyle's hospital bed. It was as confusing now as it had been then.

There was only one thing clear in her mind—she loved Trevor Dalton in ways she'd never dreamed of in all the wildest, most romantic, dreams of her youthful heart.

She loved him…loved *him*…only him.

Chapter Eight

"I want to keep them here under my supervision," Uncle Nick said at the conference Lyric and Trevor held with him, Aunt Fay and the three orphans late that afternoon.

Lyric had suggested that Jeremy accompany them to Boise during the investigation the next day. Uncle Nick vetoed the idea. "You can call if you have a question, can't you?" he asked in rather querulous tones.

"Yes. I just thought it might be easier if we had someone who knew exactly where we were going and who we were looking for."

"The police might try to nab Jeremy for kidnapping or something," Uncle Nick reminded them.

"He's of legal age to be tried as an adult, so we have to be careful."

Lyric hadn't considered that angle. Jeremy had taken two minors from their court-appointed home. Judges could sometimes be rigid about things like that, although Jeremy had been a minor himself at the time.

Complications. Life was full of them.

With the orphans staying at the ranch, it meant that she and Trevor would be making the trip to check out Jeremy's uncle on their own. She'd told Aunt Fay she would be perfectly fine going alone, but her aunt had given the elder Dalton a worried glance, and he'd nixed that idea, too.

"Two minds are better than one," he'd told them.

"What time should we leave?" she asked, giving up the argument and turning to Trevor.

"Eight. We'll get the chores done, then take off."

She nodded.

"Speaking of chores," Uncle Nick spoke up, "Travis says the hay is ready to be baled. You ever drive a baler?" he asked Jeremy.

The young man was surprised by the question. "No, sir."

"Trevor can show you how it works. Tony is going to work the cow ponies for Zack, so he knows what to do." He peered at Lyric. "Do you and Krista feel up to feeding the orphan calves this evening? Alison usually does it, but Logan isn't feeling well. He's probably teething."

Lyric realized the patriarch had made sure everyone was given a responsible job to perform. As if they were all part of the family and valued as such. Nicholas Dalton was a wise man. Except when it came to her and Trevor.

"And what are you and Aunt Fay going to be doing while we're all working our butts off?" Trevor demanded.

Ten months had passed since Lyric had last heard Trevor in his lighthearted teasing mode. Despite her worries, a smile tugged at her lips.

"The usual things," his uncle replied. "Napping, reading, maybe making out a little." He waggled his bushy eyebrows at her aunt.

The three orphans stared at the old couple with the shock that youth reserves for seniors who acted as if they still had warm blood flowing in their veins. Lyric and Trevor burst out laughing at the same instant.

"If that's your opening line," Aunt Fay said with her usual asperity, "your technique needs improving."

The twitch at the corner of her mouth gave her away, though, making Lyric laugh even more. Uncle Nick's chuckle was a pleasant counterpoint to their merriment as he admitted he might need some practice.

Her aunt pressed a hand over her mouth, shook her head, then started laughing, too.

Jeremy looked at them, then at his cousins. His expression said he thought they were all weird.

That made the youngsters laugh. Finally he, too, smiled in his serious, watchful way.

Lyric sighed contentedly. Finished with the planning session, she went to her room to change from town clothes to ranch duds in preparation for evening chores.

At the dresser mirror, she paused to check on her bruises. Her knees and collarbone still had traces of green and yellow, but the discoloration under her eyes was completely gone. The soreness had disappeared, too, unless she pressed on her kneecap in a certain way.

A trace of a smile lingered on her lips from her earlier laughter. It had been a long time since she'd laughed, really laughed, at anything.

Perhaps it was good that she and Trevor had a project to work on, she mused, a flutter of anticipation running through her at the thought of the coming trip. It would give them common ground, something to concentrate on rather than their troubles. After all, other people's woes were so much more interesting and easier to resolve than one's own.

She smiled again at her reflection, then dressed and went to find Krista. The girl and her brother were already in the paddock next to the stable. Each rode a cow pony and sat easily in the saddle.

"Where did you learn to ride?" she called out when Krista guided her mount over to the fence.

"Mom was cook at a ranch for a long time. When the owner died, his family sold the ranch to a developer. That's why we moved to town. No one needs a ranch cook anymore.''

"What did your mother do in town?''

"Waitress. It didn't pay as much, but the manager said the other cooks would quit if he hired a woman in the kitchen. That doesn't seem fair, does it?''

Lyric, seated on the fence railing, met the girl's troubled gaze. "No, it isn't.''

Krista's brown eyes, so dark they were almost black, swept over the landscape. "It's nice here,'' she said in her soft, shy manner. "I hope…I hope we can stay.''

Lyric felt the girl's longing for a home and stability tug at her own heart. "Me, too,'' she said sincerely.

She realized she was including herself in that hope.

On Thursday morning, Lyric and Trevor were on the road at eight as planned. The sky was clear for the trip.

"It's going to be hot,'' she said.

"Good for getting the hay in.''

"Yes.''

Her gaze was drawn from the way the sun gilded the pastures to his handsome profile. They were in his truck rather than her car, which she'd offered to drive. He'd declined. Men liked to be in control, she mused.

He was his serious, wary self again. She missed the laughing companion of last year, the one she'd briefly seen again yesterday when he'd teased his uncle and her aunt.

"Do you think Aunt Fay and your uncle have, uh, made out?" she asked without thinking the words over first.

"Yeah, I do."

She frowned at his certainty.

"Does that bother you?" he demanded.

"I'm not sure." She considered. "I'm wondering what my dad would say if I returned home without her."

"Did you talk to him?"

"Yes. Last night. He gave me permission to use the emergency funds and thought we should hire an attorney as an advocate for Jeremy and the kids." She hesitated. "Aunt Fay raised my dad, so he's sort of protective of her…" She trailed off, not wanting to insult Trevor's family.

"Does he think my uncle is interested in her for her money or something?" he asked coolly, taking her concern in the wrong vein just as she'd feared he would.

"No. We didn't get into anything personal, but he would want to, um, check out your family if…if…"

"If things are serious between the senior citizens?" Trevor finished for her.

"Something like that."

He cut her a sharp glance as he paused before turning onto the paved road to town. "Wouldn't you vouch for Uncle Nick?"

"Of course. He's a wonderful person. It's just that

this is a long way from Texas. Aunt Fay has never lived anywhere else."

"Yes, it is a long trip," he agreed as he made the turn. He glanced at her again as if assessing her ability to transplant from her native soil.

In a moment they passed the lake and the community of homes and businesses that had sprung up around it, then entered the small town with its one grocery, one garage, a tiny post office, a branch bank and a couple of mom-and-pop restaurants. There was one main street and a couple more running parallel to it, plus several side streets. The population was a bit over a thousand, according to the sign denoting the city limits.

"But she would be happy here," Lyric continued. "She would be happy anywhere, if she made up her mind to it."

So would I.

She longed to say the words, but knew she wouldn't like his sardonic comeback.

Would you? he would ask, then give her an amused glance laced with the cynicism she hadn't seen last year. Sighing, she wondered if she had done that to him.

Maybe she was being presumptuous about her influence. He probably didn't care what she thought. She stole another peek at his handsome profile before forcing her eyes to the passing scenery again.

Actually the area wasn't too different from her home. The sagebrush here outnumbered the cattle, which outnumbered the people. Just like Texas. The mountains were higher, though, and the winters longer and colder.

Turning to him, she said, "We don't get all that much snow in Austin. Here it must stay on the ground all winter." Her voice went up at the end in a question.

"That's right. It's a cold, hard winter. The growing season is one of the shortest in the States. A lot of people can't take it."

"Like me?" she asked softly.

His hands tightened on the steering wheel, then he shrugged as if he didn't care.

A sense of defiance, something new to her, she was discovering, brought a taunt to her lips. "I think it would depend on the reason a person moved here."

"Yeah? Such as?"

"Perhaps a job and how much one liked it," she suggested. "Or a special person and how much one wanted to be with that person."

He flashed her a mocking smile. "A man apparently has to be at death's door to be that special to you."

"That was a bit below the belt," she murmured in protest, hurt by the statement.

She saw his chest lift and fall in a heavy breath. "Okay, it was," he admitted. "I'm sorry."

"So am I," she told him. "I'm sorry I didn't explain things to you last fall. I should have, but I was afraid."

"Afraid?" Again the skepticism in his tone.

Nodding, she explained, "Everything was so new and different between us. It all happened so fast. I didn't trust the feelings...or myself."

He cast her a quick look but didn't say anything.

"Rodeo cowboys have reputations," she said, "and I didn't know you. I didn't trust you, not enough."

"Funny," he said, "how differently people view the same situation. I did trust you, you see."

She remembered his eyes at the moment that trust was broken—the puzzlement, the disbelief, the anger that flashed through those azure depths, followed by the cold, hard distrust of a person who'd been deceived.

"I know," she said softly, her heart filled with sorrow if he could just peer inside and see it.

He shrugged. "It's all water under the bridge. We have other things to worry about at the present. There's a map of the city in the door pocket. Look up the directions to the address Jeremy gave us for his uncle."

She smiled, albeit with a touch of her aunt's asperity. So much for Travis's advice to talk and clear things up between them. Maybe seduction was the best course.

Trevor stood behind Lyric while they waited for someone to answer the door. She rang the doorbell again while he continued his survey of the yard and buildings.

The place was neat. The lawn was trimmed and flowers grew in profusion in raised beds. There were odd but interesting sculptures, apparently made from junk, among the flowers and shrubs. The home was a trailer.

"Coming," an irritated voice called from inside.

A man opened the door. He was dressed in shorts, so the artificial leg below his knee was plainly visible. Like Jeremy, he had dark hair and eyes. Trevor estimated the man was in his early forties. He was a veteran who'd lost a foot due to a land mine, Jeremy had told them last night.

"Yes?" he said, his tone noncommittal as he waited for them to speak.

"Mr. Aquilon? I'm Lyric Gibson. This is Trevor Dalton. We're here about your nephew—"

"Jeremy? You know where he is?"

"Yes," Trevor said. "He's at a safe place."

The man frowned, irritation again coming to the fore. "The kid took off last year without a word. I had to tell the welfare people I didn't know where he was. They were pretty angry, like it was my fault or something."

"He did a brave thing," Lyric told the man. "I'd like to tell you about it. If you have time?"

The man hesitated. "Sure."

Stepping back, he opened the door so they could

enter, his manner still wary, but indicating a willingness to hear them out. Trevor followed Lyric inside.

The house trailer was as neat as the lawn and garden. Jeremy hadn't lived in squalor. Lyric chose a seat at a round oak table. Trevor took one, too. Aquilon propped a hip on a bar stool at the peninsula that separated the kitchen from the living room.

"Tell me what this is all about," he ordered with the confidence of a man used to being in charge.

"We found Jeremy and his two cousins in the national forest near the Dalton ranch."

"Where's that?" he asked.

"Lost Valley," Trevor told him. "The town is about an hour north of here, the ranch forty minutes west of that."

The man nodded. "What were they doing up there?"

"Living off the land." Lyric then told him the whole story of the youngster's flight to safety.

A muscle ticked in Aquilon's jaw. Bitter irony flashed across his face. "And they said my place wasn't good enough for the kids," he said roughly.

Lyric reached out and briefly touched his arm. Trevor saw sympathy on her expressive face. "How many bedrooms do you have here?" she asked.

"Two. You planning on staying the night?"

Trevor couldn't help but smile at the man's sardonic brand of humor. He decided he liked Aquilon.

Lyric shook her head, her smile one of understanding. Trevor silently sighed. He could see determination in the set of her mouth.

"Family Services couldn't have approved your place for three kids," she said. "It's too small. The rules are that each child must have his or her own private space."

"So they can be preyed on easier?"

Lyric shook her head. "Everyone needs a private retreat at times. Fortunately Antonio could lock his door. After his sister was whipped so badly, he climbed out the window and went to find Jeremy."

Jeff grinned. "I knew the kid was smart."

Lyric explained about the foundation she represented and its interest in the three orphans. "I'm going to investigate and see what we can do for them. Jeremy said you were willing to take all three?"

"Yeah. Jeremy is my only living relative. Tony and Krista's mother took him in when he was hardly more than a stripling, even though he wasn't blood kin to her. I was in service then and out of the country. How could I do less for her children?" His face darkened. "We were fine here, then someone told the welfare people. They took the two younger kids to a shelter, then put them in foster care after they said my place wasn't approved."

Trevor told him what Seth had done about custody for the three. "Uncle Nick won't put up with any nonsense about them going to some shelter," he finished.

For the first time a genuine smile appeared on the

other man's face as he gazed at Lyric. "So what happens next?" he asked.

"I hope you don't mind if I ask your neighbors questions about you," she said. "I have to have a full report to present to the judge. I personally would like to see them with someone like you. You're related to Jeremy and by extension, to the others. The problem is with the size of your home."

He frowned. "I haven't had time to build a house. My business has just turned the corner and become profitable."

"What kind of business are you in?" she asked, getting a notebook and pen from her purse.

"Junk. After my retirement, due to medical reasons—" he paused and gave his leg a glance "—I decided to make it as an artist, but I knew I needed something for cash flow. Come on, I'll show you my shop."

Trevor followed behind the other two as they left the trailer, crossed the neat garden and entered a huge barn. It was filled with a great many items in various states of repair. Or disrepair, as the case may be.

"I go to garage sales and thrift stores, but I pick up a lot of stuff at the dump, too, or from houses being torn down. This is considered a salvage operation. I take other people's junk and try to make something useful out of it. Builders come to me for moldings, mantels, things like that, for restoring homes. I sell some sculptures I've made from odds and ends."

"How interesting," Lyric said in her warm, enthusiastic way, the same as Trevor remembered from last year when he'd explained his and Zack's plans for improving their cutting horses. An odd feeling shot through him like a hot spear.

He paused to study a sculpture—a fountain, he realized after reading the tag—that was made from old oil cans with long slender spouts. Lyric and Aquilon continued their tour.

The man was in his element as he eagerly told her of his plans for expansion for his growing business.

The hot spear hit Trevor again. It took a second, but then he recognized it. Jealousy.

He silently cursed. He wasn't jealous of a crippled vet who was at least sixteen years older than Lyric…even if she was laughing in delight as the man explained one of his zanier sculptures. He cursed again, but it didn't relieve the hot burning pit in his stomach.

Knowledge sifted through the red haze that blurred his inner vision. Lyric had a soft spot for children, the homeless, the downtrodden, those who'd been hurt by life. The injured veteran and his little band of misused orphans qualified on all counts. She was fully absorbed in her self-appointed task of saving them.

And he was jealous.

So what kind of person did that make him? He shook his head. He didn't want to think about it.

Lyric noticed Trevor hung back and didn't seem interested in helping with the investigation. She listened attentively to Jeff's plans for his business and realized he didn't have the resources to build a house at the present. He needed every bit of money to establish his career.

With gentle questioning, she noted he received a veteran's pension, which gave him a nominal amount to live on, but wasn't enough to support one person, much less three more. That's where the foundation could help.

After two hours, she felt she had enough information from Jefferson Aquilon. She made sure he understood she was going to question the neighbors and asked for references he wished to include in her report.

"Thank you very much for your cooperation," she said, shaking hands with the vet, who was now relaxed and charming with them. "Ready?" she asked Trevor.

"Yes." He shook hands with Aquilon, then led the way across the yard.

"I'm going to talk to some of the neighbors before we leave," she told him. "After lunch, I have three references to visit. Then we'll see the social worker on this case."

For the rest of the day, Trevor played the mostly silent companion, staying at her side while she questioned and probed and made notes. Lunch had been at a fast-food place at her request.

At four, they had an appointment with the case

worker, an elderly woman who looked frazzled and out of sorts.

"You realize we could hold Jeremy on criminal charges?" was the first thing she said when he and Lyric were seated in her cramped office.

"Yes, and so does he," Lyric agreed, surprising Trevor with her easy manner. "You realize Krista was in danger at the foster home you had approved and had to flee? Our attorney, Seth Dalton, spoke to the county judge in Lost Valley. The presiding judge here has remanded the case to Lost Valley jurisdiction. The children were put in the custody of Nicholas Dalton."

"Mr. Dalton is a well-known and respected citizen," the case worker—Mrs. Greyling, according to the sign on her desk—admitted, "but he's surely too, uh…"

The woman clearly changed her mind about what she was going to say.

"That is," she continued, "he isn't married, and, at his age, he surely isn't interested in raising another bunch of orphans."

"He doesn't have to," Lyric said smoothly. "I'm eager to take the children myself."

"You're married and can provide a settled home?"

Mmm, the woman had one up on Lyric there. Trevor met the soft, brown eyes of his nemesis. She didn't say a word. She didn't have to. She needed his help.

Without even giving himself a second to think, he

said, "Lyric and I plan to marry soon. I own part of Seven Devils Ranch. We'll be more than able to provide the stable home Family Services' rules require."

He saw Lyric blink as shock flitted through her eyes, then it was gone. In its place was a warm glow. Her mouth trembled at the corners as she controlled a grin at the out-and-out lie.

The older woman glanced at Lyric's left hand, which had no engagement ring, sighed and slumped in her chair. "When will the happy occasion take place?" she asked skeptically, holding a pen over the open folder on her desk.

"Soon," he said. "Next month."

"At any rate," Lyric cut in before he could elaborate, "jurisdiction has now been transferred to the Lost Valley district and I've been appointed to investigate what's to be done with the children. Are you going to press charges regarding Jeremy's taking the children out of a dangerous situation?"

The woman's smile was cold. "No, I don't see any need. You two seem to have everything under control. When I get a copy of the court order, I'll close out my file."

"They may return here to live with Jeremy's uncle."

"His place isn't suitable."

"But if it had a bedroom for each child?" Lyric leaned forward and spoke in confidential tones. "I think the foundation would be willing to help with that. Mr. Aquilon has checked out as a decent, caring person so far. If his house were larger, what would you think about them staying there?''

To Trevor's amusement, the woman considered the idea, then nodded her head. ''Everything did check out okay for him to have Jeremy. But the others, well, there were rules.''

Lyric was at once sympathetic and supportive. ''I know. With your approval, I'm satisfied my opinion of Jeff isn't off base. I'll have to talk to the trustees of the foundation, but I think we will be able to help.'' She stood and held out a hand. ''Thank you so much for taking time out of your day to handle this. I feel much better about the situation now.''

Mrs. Greyling stood, too. Her manner was sardonic as she shook hands with Lyric. ''I'm glad to see this case off my plate. The department took a lot of criticism when the children disappeared and no one could find them. I'll be glad to see the situation resolved.''

They said their farewells and left the county building. ''I'd hate to ever make her angry,'' he told Lyric as they crossed the street to the public parking lot. ''I didn't much think she cared about anything but rules when we first went in, but maybe I misread her.''

''Her job is a hard one. A person has to toughen up to handle all the distress she probably sees on a daily basis. I'm not sure I could do it.''

''Yeah,'' he agreed. ''You're too softhearted.''

She gave him a knowing perusal. ''Uncle Nick said you always took in every stray animal to come along.''

"That was a long time ago. I've toughened up since then," he told her. "It's the rush hour. We may as well go have dinner while we wait for some of the city traffic to ease off. I have a favorite place here."

"Really? Maybe we can discuss our sudden engagement when we get there."

He nodded. In the truck on the way to the steak house overlooking the river, he asked the one thing that had been nagging at him for months. "Your mother said you'd set a wedding date last spring. If he'd lived, were you going to keep it?"

He braked at a red light and looked at her.

Sorrow settled on her face, and the earlier glow disappeared. "Yes," she said, so low he could barely hear the words. "Yes, I was."

The hot spear that had hit his stomach earlier landed in his throat. He nodded without speaking.

They arrived at the restaurant without another word passing between them. The sense of betrayal, the same as he'd experienced while in Texas, burned like a hot coal all the way to his soul.

Well, he'd been curious, he'd asked and he'd gotten her answer. He just wished it didn't feel like a torch turning his insides to cinders....

Chapter Nine

The restaurant already had a line. Lyric waited for Trevor to decide if they would join it. He told the hostess his name and that they would be in the bar. Taking Lyric's arm, he guided her into the quieter area.

Seated at the counter on stools, Lyric ordered iced raspberry tea, Trevor a glass of red wine. The news was on a television mounted over the bar. She stared at it while her mind ran in circles.

Understanding fully why he had declared them engaged, she worried about how to handle the situation. Finally she spoke. "Thanks for coming to my rescue with Mrs. Greyling. She wasn't very receptive to my ideas at first, but then she warmed up. I think it was the Dalton name."

"Or the engagement," he said laconically.

Lyric frowned. "Well, I don't think that made a big impression. For one thing, she didn't believe us. For another, the agency probably likes to see a marriage of several years and an older couple before approving them as foster parents."

"That's changing some as families become more diverse. If Aquilon doesn't get an okay, then Uncle Nick will. The ranch is the best place in the world for kids."

This was said with such conviction, Lyric had to smile. Trevor and his particular group of orphans had lived a happy life with their uncle. "I agree," she said softly. "My brothers and I loved it when we moved to my grandfather's place permanently."

"Your mother didn't care for it."

"You're right. I didn't realize how things were. As long as their folks stick together, kids think things are fine, even if the parents argue all the time."

"Is that what your parents did?"

She shook her head. "That's why the divorce was such a shock, I think. I truly didn't know the marriage was shaky. That's why I was so hesitant when—"

Realizing where this was taking her, she stopped. The past wasn't a good subject between them. Their drinks arrived and she took a cooling sip. Soft music surrounded them from overhead speakers. The cooled air was a welcome retreat from the July heat, which was well over ninety.

Thirty minutes passed in peaceful silence. "Dalton," the hostess called out.

"That's us," Trevor said, rising and letting her precede him into the dining room.

A funny shiver rushed over Lyric's nerves. She wasn't a Dalton, nor likely to be, she reminded herself firmly. No second chances for them.

She stared out the window toward the west. The sun was a big red ball close to the horizon. A small garden ran along the side of the building, rife with flowering plants. Bees and butterflies hovered around lavender and catmint.

No traffic noise penetrated the calm ambiance of the room. Only a low murmur of voices and music offset the peace and quiet. She wished...she wished...

"Do you know what you want?" Trevor asked.

Startled at first, she realized he was referring to the menu the hostess had given her. "Some kind of fish. I try to eat it when I'm dining out since I can't stand to cook it."

"You know how to cook?"

Her hackles rose at his skeptical tone. "Of course."

A smile brightened his face, making him so incredibly handsome, she couldn't breathe for a second.

He held up both hands. "I apologize. It's just that I've never seen you alone in the kitchen. I'm pretty handy in there myself."

His tone of false modesty didn't fool her. "Uncle

Nick pointed out that all the Dalton men know their way around the kitchen,'' she said wryly.

"Has he brought up the seduction idea yet?"

Lyric felt the heat hit her cheeks and ears.

"I see he has," Trevor murmured with a wicked gleam in his to-die-for eyes.

"I was tempted to tell him what you said about that, but I refrained. I, uh, didn't feel I needed any more of his helpful suggestions. He assured me you were an honorable man, as all the Daltons are."

The amusement left his face. His gaze drifted over her from her eyes to her lips, down her throat, back to her lips. She couldn't get her breath for a second.

"Where you're concerned, I wouldn't count on it," he said, his voice husky the way she remembered it when passion ran strongly between them. "Are we going to perpetuate the engagement story?"

She met his stare with a level one of her own. "I don't see any reason to do so. Do you?"

"Yeah," he said, so softly she could hardly hear. "Then we could do some making out of our own."

"If you're thinking of sex, it isn't going to happen again," she told him flippantly.

His eyes seemed to darken as he leaned back in the comfortable chair. A lazy smile curved the corners of his mouth. "Is that a challenge?"

She wasn't about to back down. "Take it any way you want," she invited recklessly, her nipples beading as if in anticipation. She held on to her nonchalant smile, but it was an effort.

"May I take your order?" the waitress asked politely.

Lyric ordered the salmon special she'd briefly noted on a chalkboard by the door when they came in. While Trevor placed his order, she gazed out the window again and thought of all that might have been.

They were mostly silent during the meal, which was delicious. It was deep twilight by the time they began the nearly two-hour trek back to the mountains.

"We accomplished quite a lot today," she said, going over her notes once they were on the highway. "Seth can set up an appointment to discuss our findings with the judge. We need to have a recommendation ready."

"We'll mention it in the morning to the others," he said, his eyes on the road as they left the city.

Traffic was light, more so as they went north, heading into the mountains. She put the notebook in her purse, sighed and relaxed against the seat. The sky was deep purple and navy blue. A few stars were out.

"The dreaming time," she murmured. "That's what one of the ranch hands called this time of day. He was part Apache and very old when we went to live on the ranch. All the kids loved him. He told us stories of the old days while we gathered around a tiny fire he built. He would rake through the embers and make predictions on our futures."

"What did he foretell for you?"

She smiled nostalgically. "It was the same for all

of us. We would go through trials and tribulations, we would gain wisdom because of this, and then we would live full lives and be kind to others and have lots of grandchildren.''

"Did he have lots of them?''

"No. His wife died in childbirth and he never remarried. I think he was ancient before he settled down on our place. He was very gentle with all young things.''

"Kids need someone who's gentle with them,'' Trevor said.

"Your uncle is like that.''

"Uncle Nick?'' He chuckled. "I suppose you could say so. As a kid, I wasn't too sure he wasn't one of the devils who'd escaped being turned into a mountain, especially when he caught any of us in wrong-doing.''

"Did he wallop you?''

He shook his head. "Nope, just gave us a lot of chores so we were too tired to get into mischief for a month. That cooled a lot of our wilder impulses.''

"But not all.''

He shot her a glance that had her temperature going up about a hundred degrees. "No, not all,'' he agreed.

She swallowed hard and tried not to think of the hunger he incited in her. It was no use. Longing for things she couldn't exactly name spread through her like a mischievous inner demon bent on having its way.

For the rest of the trip, she battled with herself, the

war raging from thoughts of seducing the silent man beside her to packing up and heading back to Texas before she got herself into a lot of foolish trouble. When they arrived at the ranch, she still hadn't subdued her personal devil.

Trevor promptly got out of the pickup when he killed the engine, but she sat there lost in reverie, her gaze drawn to the familiar scenery, so beautiful it made her heart ache.

The moon was bright, a silver banner flying over the peaks west of them. The mountains rose in lofty splendor, as far as a dream, as near as a wish.

"Oh," she whispered, a moan of need and of denial.

Trevor came around the truck and opened the door. He stood there and waited, his eyes never leaving her. Slowly she turned and let her legs slide downward. Holding the hand bracket, she let the rest of her body follow until her feet touched the ground. The cooler mountain air did nothing to chill her blood.

They stood there as if entranced. She wished Coyote would turn her into stone so she didn't have to hurt, to yearn for something that was never to be, but there was no reprieve for her aching heart.

Be brave, she told that unsteady organ. *Don't cry. Don't give yourself away.*

She ordered her body to go into the ranch house, but her feet didn't obey. Hearing Trevor's heavy sigh, she realized he was fighting the same battle she was.

Slowly, so slowly, she lifted her face until she

could meet his gaze. When he reached for her, she didn't resist. Instead she gave a soft moan and lifted her arms.

"Damn," he muttered just before his mouth closed on hers. It was a groan of surrender.

The kiss was too much...and not enough. It was everything. It was nothing, compared to what her heart wanted from him.

She shook her head slightly. Trying to figure things out only confused her more. She closed her mind to the troubling thoughts and simply gave herself to the moment.

"Hungry for you," Trevor murmured, breathing fire along her neck as he trailed greedy kisses there. It wasn't air he needed, but *her*...the taste of her, the feel of her.

"Trevor," she whispered.

He loved the sound of it. "Say it again," he demanded.

She pulled away slightly and gazed into his eyes, her eyes rich dark pools in the moonlight. He wanted to dive into those honeyed depths and never come up.

"Trevor."

He heard promises in the word. His heart did a joyful dance. Even if the promises were a lie, he wanted to believe them at this moment...had to believe them.

Lyric held his intense stare, letting him search inside her for answers to the questions between them.

She tried to find words, but she feared there was no bridge to the trust he'd once given her so freely.

When he frowned and started to draw back, she couldn't bear it. Tightening her embrace, she pressed into him. "I love the feel of you. The hard sinewy strength. The gentleness. Always the gentleness."

He pressed his face into her hair and spoke in a rough growl, "I don't always want to be gentle with you. Sometimes I want to crush you against me so hard it would be impossible to separate us."

His low laughter was cynical, mocking the sentiment, tearing her heart into raw strips of longing.

But when he kissed her again, the gentleness was there, holding the fierce need in check. Raking her fingers into his hair, she responded wildly, passionately.

Her breathing deepened, became shallow, stopped as they exchanged a thousand kisses with a thousand nuances of feeling in them, replacing the words she couldn't say. At last she had to bury her face against his neck and rest.

"I've missed you," she said, unable to resist tasting the skin above his collar. "I don't think I had ever really missed anyone. Until you."

"You could have come to me," he reminded her.

This wasn't a good topic for them. She lifted her head and searched blindly for his mouth. He didn't withhold his touch. His lips ravaged hers in tender forays. She writhed against him, the hunger too great to hide.

Trevor loved the feel of her breasts, the points contracted into hard buds of passion. He loved the way she caressed along his back and over his hips. He moved slightly and made an adjustment to ease the constriction of his briefs on the erection he couldn't disguise.

She made a low sound and rubbed against the long hard ridge, a sweet, feminine invitation to come to her.

"Darling," she said. "My darling."

And everything he'd ever wanted was in the word.

"You could tempt me beyond reason," he told her, trying to hold on to sanity even as it slipped from his grasp.

"I want to." She cupped his face in her hands. "I want to make you forget everything but us...*this.*"

She wanted so much more, but passion was a start, the first truss of the bridge over the river of caution she sensed in him. "We can share this," she whispered, filled with the greatest tenderness she'd ever known.

Trevor was silent for a moment, but he knew he was fighting a losing battle. The hunger in both of them was too great to resist.

And did he really want to? some wiser part of him asked, resigning itself to the temptation of her mouth, her body, her passion.

"No," he murmured, giving the inevitable answer.

"No?" she echoed.

''Not to you,'' he quickly said, moving against her, feeling the alluring sway as she responded. ''Come.''

Taking her hand, he escorted her into the house, turned off the night-light on the old-fashioned hurricane lamp and led her along the hall and into his room. He closed the door behind them, then waited....

Lyric didn't hesitate. She clicked the lock into place, then stepped into his arms again. ''Need you,'' she whispered, the wildness returning and sweeping reason before it like a storm wind off He-Devil mountain.

His hands went to her neat white blouse. He tried not to appear the callow youth, but his fingers trembled and he fumbled a bit as he undressed her. He muttered a curse.

Her smile flashed in the dark, pleasing him. He felt her hands on his shirt, moving rapidly from button to button. He quickly finished his task.

Pushing the silky blouse off her shoulders, he followed its downward trail, his lips touching between her breasts, then along her torso until the blouse was free of her arms.

He tossed it to a chair, stripped his shirt and threw it in the same direction. Slipping a finger under the front of her bra, he followed the band to the back. There he found the hooks and quickly dispensed with them. With a movement of her shoulders, the material slipped from her. He laid it on the chair with their shirts.

"You're beautiful." He bent to her breasts and lavished kisses over the impertinent tips that seemed to demand his attention. He chuckled when she trembled and grabbed hold of his shoulders to keep from falling.

He was feeling a bit weak in the knees, too. Swinging her into his arms, he carried her to his bed and laid her on it after tossing the comforter out of the way. He removed her shoes, then kicked his off. Aware of her eyes on him, he unfastened the belt, hook and zipper on the dress slacks and stripped them, along with the confining briefs, from his body.

When she ran a hand up and down his thigh, then his hip, he gritted his teeth and held on. "Keep that up, and I'll be forced to ravish you on the spot," he warned.

Lyric smiled at the half playful, half serious tone. "I'm overdressed," she complained softly.

"Yeah. We can fix that."

He bent over her and quickly disposed of the rest of her clothing. She closed her eyes and moved toward him, her hand finding the hard staff. She kissed the tip and felt the muscles of his buttocks clench.

"Lyric," he said on a groan.

"I've never…you did this to me…."

She wanted to bring him exquisite pleasure, to bring him to the exploding point again and again. "I want to make you crazy," she said and laughed, then began the task.

"You do," he told her, running his fingers through

her hair. "Ahh," he whispered, "I won't last a second."

He pushed her against the pillow and lay down, his leg closing over hers and tucking her in close to him. Resting on an elbow, he explored her body thoroughly while their mouths played lovers' games.

"You're ready," he said, stroking her intimately.

"What was your first clue?" she demanded, and nipped his bottom lip, her mood sensual and teasing now.

"This," he said huskily, touching her lips with one finger, then licking the sweet dew of passion from her.

Lyric opened her thighs and captured the rigid staff, then slid against him, feeling the slick moisture feed the hunger between them.

"Come to me," she demanded.

As one he rolled them so she was on her back and he loomed over her. He resisted her effort to open her legs and bring him inside. "Not yet," he said. "I haven't had near enough of you. I want to hear you gasp and whisper my name and croon those little demanding noises you make when you want me so bad you can't stand it."

"I want you that way now."

He clicked the bedside lamp on. "I want to see you. I want you to look at me when you go over the edge. I want you to know who's making you feel this."

She blinked in the sudden light, then holding his

gaze, she told him, "I know who you are. You're the only one who makes me feel this way—wild and primitive…and free in a way I can't explain. You make me soar," she finished softly, reaching up to brush the wave off his forehead. "You, and only you."

"Who am I?" he asked with that trace of cynicism she knew she'd brought to him.

"Trevor Dalton," she said firmly. "Trevor. My love."

His chest rose against hers, then he shook his head as if he didn't believe her. "Leave emotion out of it. Passion is enough."

She nodded and smiled. "It's a start."

He didn't argue, but his gaze warned her not to count on more from him. Pulling his head down to her mouth, she tried to remind him of all the things they had once shared and could share again, if he would but trust her as he had when they first met.

His kisses became more demanding. Her caresses became more heated. They touched everywhere until the deep, sweet hunger overrode all else.

"Wait," he murmured, breathing heavily as he pulled away from her.

He quickly opened the bedside drawer, then secured the condom before coming back to her. Eagerly she opened herself to him and gasped as he came inside, melding them into one. "Perfect," she told him.

He smiled, then warned her, "Don't move."

"Have to," she said, and held her breath as sensation after sensation surged through her. "Now, my darling, now."

"All right," he whispered. "Let's take it all."

He gave her ecstasy wrapped in a rainbow, passion shot with moonbeams and clouds of stardust. He gave her joy and wonder and fulfillment.

She clung to him desperately, shamelessly and felt his passion in a throbbing release in the very center of her being. "So wonderful," she said as they drifted back to earth after their sojourn in heaven.

"Yeah, it is that," he agreed.

She caught the note of weariness in him as if he'd just returned from a long, dangerous trip. His expression was solemn when she studied him for a long moment.

"Do you regret it?" she asked.

He didn't answer right away. "How could I?" he finally said in a light tone. "It was the most intense pleasure I've ever experienced."

He wasn't going to give her love words. She hadn't expected them, but still, she missed them. A bridge was built one span at a time, she reminded her impatient heart. She would win his trust again and then...then she would steal his heart right away.

She laughed and hugged him close. "For me, too," she said, closing her eyes as sleep crept softly over her.

Trevor studied the curious mix of bliss and turmoil

this woman incited in him. He was close to losing himself in her again.

How close? Right on the edge of the abyss.

He wanted to go on over, he realized. He wanted to return to last year and start from there, with nothing between them but the growing need to be together, to touch and kiss and discover the things that lovers needed to know about each other.

Feeling her softness, listening to her breathe, he experienced a need so deep, so elemental to his being, he was afraid to delve into it and see how far down it went.

Restless now and far from sleep, he rose, disposed of the protection he'd remembered to use and pulled on a pair of sweats. Slipping into the bathroom, he washed up, then stood there in the dark, taking in the quiet of the house and thinking of all the generations who'd made their home on the ranch.

A picture of Lyric holding his nephew came to him. It would be a good life here with relatives all around to love and watch after a child, to help a kid grow up strong and secure in that love.

That's what he wanted, but was Lyric the woman to fit that dream?

Opening the door, he stepped into the hall and stopped.

"Hello," Lyric's aunt said cordially, as if they were at a tea party or something. "Did you and Lyric have a successful trip to Boise?"

"Uh, yes," he said, having to dig through his mind for the reason for the trip.

He saw her eyes glance toward his bedroom door, which, thankfully, he'd closed behind him. Then she looked at Lyric's door, which was open.

The moonlight fell across the bed, disclosing the covers neatly made up, the bed unused.

"Uh," he said, trying to come up with somewhere else she could be that sounded plausible.

"Shh," the older woman said. She tightened the belt on her robe and gave him a cryptic smile. "Let's let the night keep its secrets."

He nodded and tried to look as wise and inscrutable as a Buddha.

Aunt Fay touched his arm lightly, gave him another gentle smile that reminded him of Lyric, then went into her room. Trevor did the same.

After locking the door, he stood there in the darkness, his gaze fastened on the woman who slept in his bed. They'd made love—twice now—but he'd never slept with her.

He thought of coming into the house at the close of a long, hard day, perhaps after nursing a mare through a difficult birth, and silently undressing, mindful of the woman who peacefully slept in their shared bed.

The bed would be warm when the tired man settled into it, again being careful not to disturb the woman. Perhaps she would rouse and give a welcoming sigh as she moved closer to him. He thought of spooning his body to hers and holding her, simply holding her.

A husband's pleasure with his wife didn't always mean sex, Uncle Nick had explained, although that was part of it.

There was also the joy of companionship, of having someone who was always on your side, even when you were wrong and she told you so. There was the contentment of knowing this woman had entrusted her life, her body and her heart to your keeping, and only she could deny them to you.

With a smile Trevor went to the bed. For the moment he was content to stand there and listen to Lyric's soft breathing. It was odd, this contentment, this peace that reached right down inside him. It was like being joyful with the effervescence muted to gentle, golden bubbles.

A husband's pleasure.

Placing a hand over his suddenly pounding heart, he shook his head slightly, confused by his thoughts and the emotions that filled him.

Finally he stripped off the pants and slid into bed. Lyric turned to her side and cupped her body against his. He put an arm over her waist and molded his length to hers. He probably should send her to her room so there would be no awkwardness in the morning....

He didn't move.

Well, he always woke early, before Uncle Nick nowadays. Pressing his face into her sweet-scented hair, he admitted he wasn't ready to let her go. This pleasure, that of a lover, not a husband, he reminded himself, might never come again. This one time he wanted to sleep with her in his arms and not have to think of anything else.

Maybe it was the cowardly way out, but he wasn't ready to deal with the problems that seemed to plague their waking hours. With a tenderness he'd never experienced, he smoothed Lyric's hair when she tucked her head under his chin and sighed as if she, too, were filled with happiness.

They would have this night. Tomorrow could take care of itself.

Just before he went to sleep, he wondered why the older woman had been in the hallway at that hour. There'd been no one up and about when he and Lyric had arrived. And she'd been going toward her room. If she'd gotten up and decided to have a snack, he would have noticed a light in the kitchen when he'd crossed the hall on his way to the bathroom. Why had she been wandering around in the dark?

Sleepwalking was one answer. There were others he could think of. A smile tugged at the corners of his mouth.

Let the night keep its secrets.

Chapter Ten

Lyric woke with a start the next morning. She realized at once where she was. And that it was getting light outside. Sitting up, holding the sheet over her nude body—she'd never before in her life slept naked!—she gathered her courage and looked at Trevor.

"Good morning," he said. "Sorry to wake you. I was trying to be quiet."

She glanced at the window. "The sun is up."

"Yeah. I overslept. It's almost six. I'm usually up around five."

His smile was solemn, but it filled her heart with, oh, so many things—joy, anguish, hope, despair. She watched as he pulled on jeans over the blue briefs, then a T-shirt and work shirt over that.

She couldn't tell what he was thinking, and that bothered her. After the intimacy of the night, she felt a closeness she'd never before experienced with another person. If there'd been no past between them...

"There's a robe on the back of the closet door if you want to use it," he told her.

There was a quietness in him, in his way of moving, as if he was in a sickroom and being considerate of the patient. Maybe he was being cautious about them, waiting to see her reaction this morning?

To her surprise, he put away his shoes and clothing that had been left scattered around the room last night and folded hers and stacked them on the chair. He placed her shoes nearby.

"You're very neat," she said in approval, smoothing her hair with her fingers and giving him a warm smile.

"Uncle Nick."

She understood completely. As a child, she would have done anything to please her great-aunt, who had taken the place of her father's parents in their lives. "Aunt Fay had very clear standards she expected from herself and others. My brothers and I tried not to disappoint her."

He sat on the side of the bed and pulled his boots on, then turned to her. "Speaking of your aunt, she and I met in the hall last night. Your bedroom door was open and you weren't in bed."

Lyric felt her heart give a gigantic lurch. "Did you tell her where I was?"

His somber smile flashed again. "She didn't ask."

Lyric nodded. "She rarely offers advice and she doesn't interfere…usually," she added. "She did connive with your uncle to bring me here. She said I had grieved long enough and it was time to put the past behind."

Trevor studied her for a long ten seconds. "Have you?"

Holding his gaze, she nodded.

She saw the hesitation in him before he leaned close, as if he would say something more but he didn't. He smelled of toothpaste and shampoo, she noted, and the aftershave he always used. She inhaled deeply, taking his essence into her. When she slid her arms around his neck, she felt the sheet fall away.

He kissed her lightly on the lips, then the neck and finally her breasts, making the nipples contract to points. She rubbed his back, loving the strength in those steely muscles, the warmth of his body through his clothing, the sweet teasing of his lips as he roamed from one place to another, all of them exciting. She pressed her face into his shoulder, wanting him and, oddly, wanting to cry.

"I'd better get busy," he murmured huskily, "or Trav will be wondering where the heck I am and if I'm going to do any work today."

"Are you cutting hay?"

"Yeah." He stood, stretched and yawned. "We have thirty acres still waiting for a first cutting. If we're lucky, we'll get another one in September or maybe October. Unless it snows.''

"We roll ours instead of baling," she told him.

"We use the supersize square bales for hay and store them in three sheds on the winter pastures. We roll straw and store it on the north side of the stable under plastic.''

She nodded, feeling very wifely as they discussed the chores to be done. Whether in Texas or Idaho, ranching was similar. Besides, a person could learn new things and adapt to new situations.

Glancing at the clock, he smiled slightly and headed for the door. After he was gone, Lyric stretched, feeling as sinuous as a cat, then rose, pulled on the robe he'd mentioned and made up the bed. Her emotions were strange this morning—half glad and half sad. She didn't understand herself, much less one enigmatic Dalton male.

Gathering her clothing, she slipped out his door and into her room without being seen.

Trevor handed his twin the bar of soap at the stable sink. It was Tuesday, and they'd spent the morning in the alfalfa field, just as they had yesterday. Now they were washing up for lunch.

He glanced out the window toward the house. Lyric would be there, helping their relatives get the meal on the table.

After Friday night he'd wondered if she would come to him again. On Saturday, when they'd turned in after the news, she'd paused at her door, hesitation in her manner but an invitation in her smile.

He'd taken her up on it, as eager as a foal to run and play in the new spring grass. Since then, they had stayed either in his room or hers.

Four nights.

His blood heated rapidly and he had to direct his thoughts away from the passion they shared.

This Thursday the family would join Seth in court for the hearing on the orphans. He and Lyric and the runaways, the uncle and the aunt needed to plan a strategy. They had discussed several ideas, but nothing seemed a sure thing.

Lyric was determined to adopt the whole bunch, if all else failed. Uncle Nick thought the judge would let the youngsters live at the ranch, no questions asked, but one never knew about the courts.

"Have you noticed Uncle Nick this past week?" Travis asked, breaking into his thoughts.

"In what way?"

"Well," Travis said, "for one thing, he's as frisky as a colt in the clover."

"Yeah, he seems pretty happy."

"He takes Lyric's aunt to town a lot."

"They have lunch at the lodge or one of the local restaurants. He's showing her the sights," Trevor told his brother, who seemed worried about the situation.

"You think there's something serious going on?"

Trevor tore a shop towel off the roll and dried his face, hands and forearms. "Yeah. Don't you?"

"He's seventy-one and has had a heart attack. You don't think...I don't know...maybe we'd better ask Beau about a man that age and in his condition—"

"If you're referring to sex, what better way to go than enjoying yourself?" Trevor asked. He glanced at the ranch house and wished he and Lyric could have the afternoon to themselves. Not a chance, he told his perky libido.

Travis narrowed his eyes and studied him. "You've been different since Lyric and her aunt arrived, too. First you were quiet and introspective, maybe angry that she was here. Now you're quiet and introspective but there's an eagerness to get back to the house. Did you two resolve things?"

"Good question, bro," he said, aiming for a light tone but hearing the grim edge to his own words. He shrugged. "I don't know the answer."

"Damn," Travis muttered, tossing the damp towel into the trash bin when he finished washing up. "I'd like to say something profound, like 'trust your heart,' but I don't know if that's the right thing to do. Uncle Nick, no doubt, would have sage advice on the subject."

"He's already told Lyric to seduce me." Trevor gave a brief, sardonic chuckle.

Trav flashed him a quizzing glance. "Has she?"

Trevor peered at his bedroom window as they crossed the quadrangle to the ranch house. "We've been sleeping together since Friday night," he admitted.

To his surprise, his twin grinned. "Well, okay!" he said, like it was a big deal or something.

"We haven't talked about the future," Trevor quickly added to quell any expectations. "They've been here two weeks. They leave in a week and two days."

He knew because he'd checked the calendar that morning. A heaviness settled in him. Odd, but when he was with Lyric it lightened, as if the golden bubbles kept it afloat, but when he was away from her, all the doubts came back and, with them, the load on his spirits.

"Ask her to stay," Travis suggested softly.

"For how long?"

His twin tapped him on the chest. "For however long your heart tells you."

Trust that unreliable organ again? "Ha," he said.

Smiling wisely, Travis held the door to the ranch house open and let him go first. "Coward," he muttered.

Trevor frowned. He scowled even more when he got inside and discovered Lyric had gone to town with his twin's wife, Alison. They were meeting Honey, his other sister-in-law, plus Amelia and Shelby, both married to his cousins, for lunch and a meeting of the Historical Society.

"Maybe I should warn Lyric about getting roped in on committees and community activities," he told her aunt, going into the kitchen to help her with the glasses of tea or milk she was pouring. "Before she knows what's happening, she'll be up to her neck in do-gooder projects.''

The older woman looked at him with eyes that were very similar to her niece's. She said, ''Lyric will always aid those who need her help. She not only has a tender heart but a strong sense of social justice. Any man who considers a life with her should know that.''

''That he'll come second to everyone else who needs her?''

The aunt shook her head as if impatient with him. ''Those she loves will come first in her heart and her loyalty, but she will tend to spread herself thin. She has yet to learn she can't be all things to all people who need her. Her ideals are high. So are the standards she sets for herself. Her husband may have to remind her at times that he, too, needs her.''

He couldn't imagine asking a woman for a scrap of attention. That seemed the ultimate insult.

''He'll have to do so without anger or recriminations. His heart will have to be big, very big,'' she finished and walked out, leaving him standing there alone, trying to sort through all the suggestions he was getting on his love life of late.

He realized he had a week and two days left to figure it out.

''Are we eating here?'' Lyric asked in surprise when Alison stopped in front of Amelia's B and B.

''Yes. Amelia needs to stay close to the house during the day, especially when she has guests.'' Alison leaned into the back of the station wagon and unsnapped the infant from the car seat. His face puckered in displeasure at being disturbed from his nap.

"Shh," the young mother murmured and rocked him in her arms until he quieted.

Lyric carried the diaper bag inside. She was a bit nervous about being around so many Dalton wives at one time, although she didn't know why. The ones she'd met were very nice. They had all been cordial to her.

And a bit speculative about her and Trevor, she admitted. She felt that way herself.

"Hi, there. Come in," Amelia greeted them when they went inside. She lowered her voice when she saw the baby had fallen back asleep. "I've set up a playpen in the back sitting room for Logan, if that's all right."

"Perfect," Alison whispered, heading down the hall.

"Hello. Glad you could join us," Amelia continued when they were alone. "Here, put your stuff on the side table. We'll eat at that table by the window. I'm going to get the food and put it on the sideboard so we can help ourselves."

Lyric put her purse and the baby's bag on the table. A round table had already been set for six people.

She followed Amelia into the kitchen. "Everything looks delicious," she told her hostess.

Amelia was married to Seth, the attorney cousin who was helping her with the Aquilon case. Alison and the baby belonged to Travis, the twin. She was getting the Dalton family sorted out and in place, she realized, just when it was nearly time to return to Austin.

"Hi, how were your classes?" Amelia said, her gaze going past Lyric.

Lyric turned and recognized the lithe dancer she'd met at the barbecue last weekend. Honey was Zack's wife. She was pregnant, although one couldn't tell it from her slender frame. Lyric wondered if the news was a secret.

"Great," Honey told them. "Hi, Lyric. Nice to see you again." She plopped down on a high stool and sneaked a stuffed mushroom. "I'm starved," she announced.

"Seth tells me you're eating for two. How far along are you? Do you have a due date yet?"

Honey shook her head. "I'm about six weeks and should be due around the end of March. Zack has already told the whole county. The ones he missed, Uncle Nick clued in."

Lyric laughed with Amelia and the mother-to-be.

"So when are you and Seth starting a family?" Honey asked Amelia, choosing a carrot stick for her next item.

"We wanted a year together." Amelia grinned. "But last month we decided to start trying, in case it takes a while."

"Well," Honey murmured with wicked glee, "if

you have any problems, I'm sure Uncle Nick will give you advice."

"He will," Alison said, coming into the kitchen from putting the baby down. She gave Honey a hug. "I have to admit I run to him each time Logan gets a sniffle. He's always calm and he always has a remedy."

Chatting gaily, the four women placed the food on the sideboard near the dining table. "Shelby will be here soon," their hostess told them.

"Who's the other place for?" Honey asked.

"Peggy Sue," Amelia said.

"Is she a Dalton wife, too?" Lyric asked, wondering if she'd missed one.

The others burst into laughter. Amelia answered. "She's in her seventies, I would guess. She taught school here for eons and is head of the Historical Society. Mmm, she's a distant Dalton cousin, but she's also Shelby's cousin…second cousin…or is that first cousin, once removed?"

"First cousin, once removed, I think," Honey answered. "Shelby's mom explained all that when Shelby and Beau were married, but I get mixed up on the number of removes."

"Do I hear my name?" an amused feminine voice called from the back hallway.

Shelby was a nurse who'd come to town looking for clues to her birth parents. She'd found both her past and her future here in Lost Valley, if Lyric correctly recalled the information Trevor had given her last year.

Beau Dalton had married his nurse as soon as he could talk her into it. He also had a son from a former relationship that apparently hadn't worked out. The boy lived with the couple.

Pleased that she had all this figured out, Lyric relaxed as Shelby entered the great room along with an older woman whose face crinkled into a thousand lines when she smiled at the group. Amelia introduced Lyric and the newcomers.

"So you met Trevor last year," the older woman said. Her manner was affectionate as she mentioned the last bachelor Dalton. "That scamp. It's time he settled down. He's wonderful with babies."

Heat rushed up Lyric's neck. She felt it in her cheeks and ears. Did everyone in the valley know when and where they'd met? And that they were sleeping together?

The heat increased, sweeping down her body in a tidal wave of remembered ardor.

"I've seen him with his nephew," she said, and tried not to think of him holding another baby, *their* baby.

"Let's sit, shall we?" Amelia suggested. "I'll bring the platters over and pass them around. I think that would be the easiest."

The women took seats at the table while their hostess served them chicken salad and pasta dishes along with veggies from the garden Lyric could see out the window.

"This place seems lovelier each time I see it," she told Amelia. "In fact, the whole town seems to be bursting with flowers."

"And beards," Honey added. "Pioneer Days start in August. There's a prize for the longest beard grown since the first of the year."

"I noticed that when Trevor and I were in town," Lyric admitted. "I thought maybe it was a local custom or religious group that lived around here. None of the Dalton men are taking part?"

"Due to vanity," Shelby explained. "The Dalton men aren't very hirsute. Their beards are downright scraggly."

"Seth was going to grow a handlebar mustache for that part of the contest, but when he saw how much work it was to keep it neat—all that trimming and combing and waxing—he decided he didn't want the prize that bad," Amelia said with a confiding grin.

"What's the prize?" Honey asked.

"A bull," Peggy Sue, whose last name was Pickford, told them. "As if we don't have quite enough of those around."

Lyric found herself laughing at tales of the local population as well as the tourists who passed through on their way to Hells Canyon recreational areas or taking the scenic route over to Yellowstone.

"Now for the big event," Peggy Sue said at the

end of the meal. She retrieved a rather hefty book from her purse and held it up.

The Dalton wives exclaimed in pleasure. Lyric saw by the subtitle it was a history of the county, based upon oral traditions and county records. The binding was burgundy, the lettering and trim gold.

"We worked on this most of last year," Shelby explained. "It's the Historical Society's pride and joy, also our main fund-raiser. We plan to sell them during the Pioneer Days celebration."

Lyric was fascinated, especially when she got a turn to skim through the pages and saw there was a long section on the Daltons in the founders' chapter.

Before she quite knew how it happened, she was busily planning the coming year's activities with the group.

"Watch it," Shelby advised, giving Lyric a friendly nudge with her elbow as she passed around fruit tarts for dessert. "Peggy Sue will have you heading up a committee, and you'll have to stay the whole year."

"I never pressure anyone," the older woman said in a righteous manner that brought whoops of laughter from the others.

Although Lyric smiled just as much while they had the tarts and coffee, she was glad when the meeting ended shortly after that. Alison fed Logan and changed his diaper before they got on the road.

"He's such a good baby," Lyric said in crooning

tones as he gurgled and tried to grab her finger while she tickled him under the chin.

Alison nodded. ''Most of the time. There are moments when he can be a little devil.'' She laughed softly. ''Takes after his father. And uncles and cousins.''

''Once removed,'' Lyric added.

''Whatever.''

On the way to the ranch, Lyric stared at the scenery as if it were new and different. Her heart beat faster as they went under the log entrance at the ranch driveway.

The temperature was in the eighties, and only a few clouds dotted the sky. Every blade of grass seemed to shine as if polished to a high sheen.

Lyric was aware of Alison's gaze when the lovely young mother stopped at her house and turned off the engine.

''It's beautiful, isn't it?'' she murmured, looking at the peaks to the west. ''Travis found me in the woods looking for my sister last year. He thought I was lost. I was, in a way. I needed to find a life of my own.''

''And you found it here?''

''Yes, but not without difficulty. Travis lost his childhood sweetheart and son during a premature birth. He blamed himself. Then he had to deliver my sister's baby in an SUV during a storm. The Dalton men tend to withdraw into themselves when they're hurting.''

Lyric thought of the quiet she sensed in Trevor, as

if he'd gathered a cloak of stillness around his inner being that nothing could penetrate.

"How do you reach them when they do that?" she asked.

Alison shook her head, her smile becoming pensive. "I think they have to come out of it on their own. When Travis showed up at a fund-raiser for my father, I thought he'd realized he couldn't live without me, but he would have left if we hadn't come face-to-face."

"What happened?"

"He admitted he'd come to ask me to marry him, but seeing me at the party with its rich trappings and elegantly dressed people made him change his mind. So I asked him to take me away from all that. He realized I meant it."

"And now you're living happily ever after," Lyric concluded the tale.

"Well, we have our moments, but mostly, yes, we're very happy. I'd like that for Trevor." She gave Lyric a cryptic smile. "I think you're the woman he fell in love with last year. I think he still feels that way."

"He doesn't trust me. There were problems—"

"I know about the old friend and the engagement that existed only in his mind…and perhaps his mother's."

"And my mother's," Lyric told her. "She was for it."

"Maybe she thought it was a way of keeping you

close. Didn't you stay with her a lot after the divorce?''

Lyric nodded. "She seemed terribly lonely."

"I learned that a person has to decide her own future," Alison said softly. "This is unasked-for advice, but you remind me of myself a year ago, trying to make everyone happy and solve all problems. It can't be done. You need a base of happiness for yourself. I think, for you, that's Trevor...if I'm reading the signs correctly."

When she gave Lyric an expectant glance, Lyric nodded. "I fell in love with him nearly at first sight. It was confusing because I'm not usually an impetuous person. I didn't trust my feelings."

"And now?"

Lyric took a deep breath, released it. "I love him totally, in ways I didn't know existed before we met."

"Good. Have you told him?" Without waiting for an answer, Alison slid from the station wagon, retrieved the sleeping baby and went inside.

Lyric followed. At Alison's instructions, she laid a blanket on the living-room floor, then she sat down and played with Logan while his mom went to get a bottle.

From the kitchen Lyric heard Alison speak, then a male voice answer. Travis, she assumed, although it was nearly impossible to tell his voice from his twin's. Even so, her pulse sped up a bit.

"'This little piggie went to market,'" she said,

wiggling the baby's big toe and going through the nursery rhyme.

When she leaned over, he grabbed her hair and tried to taste it. Laughing she blew raspberries on his cheek and neck, then on his belly.

He laughed in delight and waved his arms, then touched her face in little pats before trying to get her hair to his mouth once again. His eyes were already changing from the smoky blue of babies' eyes to the deep true blue of the Dalton clan. Ah, but he was going to be a heartbreaker.

If Trevor married the Nordic blonde on the neighboring ranch, their children's eyes would be blue, too.

She found that idea caused a shaft of burning hurt to land inside her and shied away from it. The baby explored her lips with his tiny fingers, his touch gentle like another Dalton she could name. He stared into her eyes as if spellbound, then he gave her a big smile.

"What a lover you're going to be," she told him, gathering him into her arms. "You have so many male relatives to learn from, the girls won't have a chance."

"Maybe we can learn a thing or two from him," a masculine baritone said. "Logan seems to have won your heart without a lot of trying on his part. What's his secret?"

Lyric met Trevor's penetrating gaze. "His eyes, I think. He looks at whoever is holding him as if that person is the sole being in his entire universe. It's very flattering, not to mention ego enlarging.''

Trevor chuckled and settled on the floor beside her. She noted he'd left his boots at the door. The Dalton men were very good about that. He smelled of alfalfa and sunshine, with maybe a whiff of diesel fuel thrown in.

Someone should bottle it as an aphrodisiac, she mused, going dizzy at his nearness.

''Hey, little man, how ya doing today?'' He tickled his nephew under the arm, eliciting a squeal of laughter. ''Got something for you.''

Logan was clearly thrilled when he spotted the bottle of formula. Lyric prepared to shift the infant to his uncle.

With one arm Trevor expertly took the baby and tucked him against his chest. Logan took the nipple eagerly.

''Yeah, that's the way I feel about it, too,'' Trevor murmured in approval, then he gave her a sexy grin.

Lyric's heart fluttered like a drunk butterfly's. She leaned against his arm. ''I would like a baby,'' she said, then was astounded. She didn't know where the words came from, certainly not from her sane, rational self. ''With you,'' she added, then bit into her lip, appalled at how that must sound.

He smiled in the teasing way she loved. ''Sorry,'' he said with mock regret. ''Uncle Nick is strict about things like that.''

They looked into each other's eyes for a long minute. Lyric sensed the stillness in him…as if he waited for something…

She opened her mouth, the words on the tip of her tongue. *Tell him,* the impetuous imp inside her urged.

Laughter erupted from the kitchen as Alison and Travis shared some amusement. Then there was silence…and more silence. Lyric looked at the nursing baby as yearning filled her.

"Here," Trevor said abruptly. "I've got work to do."

He laid Logan in her arms, handed her the bottle and rose in one fluid motion. She heard him speak to the others in the kitchen, then the sound of the door opening and closing.

She wondered, had they been completely alone, what he might have done and what he might have said.

Chapter Eleven

"Lyric?"

Lyric glanced over at Krista with a smile. They were feeding the orphaned animals. "Yes?"

"Tomorrow is Thursday."

Lyric knew at once what the girl was referring to. "Our court day, yes."

"Do you think the judge will let us stay here?"

Krista's eyes were filled with equal parts hope and fear. Although Lyric wanted to assure her that all would be well, she didn't. The outcome of the case wasn't up to her.

"I hope so." She stepped outside the gate when her calf had finished the formula in the bucket, and leaned on the fence, her mood pensive. "But we don't know what the judge will decide."

Krista held her bucket so the calf could get the last few sips. "They'll separate us this time," the girl said with fatalistic surety. "That's what they do when you get into trouble. They'll send me and Tony to different places and won't tell us where."

"You both have the phone number here at the ranch. Uncle Nick will want to know what's happening. I'll give you my number and address in Austin. We can write to each other. So can you and Tony if you do go to different places."

But that wouldn't happen, not if she could prevent it. She had the whole Dalton gang behind her.

Krista nodded and exited the calf pen. Her expression said she was resigned to the worst. "If we can't stay with Uncle Jeff, then Tony and I want to live here with Uncle Nick and all you guys. Do you think Jeremy will go to prison for running away with us?"

Lyric looped an arm around the thin shoulders as they walked to the supply room at the stable. "Well, since Tony went to Jeremy for help, I don't see how anyone can hold that against your cousin. Uncle Nick will make sure the judge understands the situation."

A smile broke out over the girl's solemn face. "He's funny, isn't he? He sounds like an ol' bear, but he's really nice. He taught me and Tony how to play cards. Me and him beat Aunt Fay and Tony."

"He and I..." Lyric began, stopped, then said, "Never mind, it isn't important right now."

"He and I beat Aunt Fay and Tony," Krista said, correcting herself and giving Lyric a pleased grin.

"Uncle Jeff said we had to learn grammar so people wouldn't think we were stupid."

"A wise man, just like Uncle Nick."

Leading the way, Lyric and Krista mixed up more formula in the buckets and returned to their chores. That afternoon Uncle Nick sent them to the hay field in the station wagon.

Lyric couldn't keep from staring at the display of prime male flesh in the field. She'd expected Trevor, Travis, Jeremy and Tony, but Zack was also there, and another man instantly recognizable as a Dalton.

"Hey, look who's here," this latter worker called out.

"Hi," Lyric said, getting out of the car. "I'm Lyric. This is Krista. You must be Beau, the doctor?"

"Right."

Tractor engines were shut down and the other men joined the girls under the shade of a huge old oak. Krista helped Lyric pass around glasses of iced tea or lemonade, along with chocolate chip and peanut butter cookies still warm from the oven. She and Krista had made them.

"Man, that was good," Travis said after downing the whole glass of lemonade. Krista poured him another from the icy thermal cooler on the back of the station wagon.

"So is this," Trevor added, savoring a peanut butter cookie. "I could eat the whole bag."

"Just try it," Zack threatened. He grabbed the plastic bag from his brother, got a handful of cookies and tossed the bag to Jeremy. With an impressive leap, Trevor retrieved the treat when Jeremy threw it to Beau.

"You boys behave yourselves," Lyric intoned in a deep voice, waggling her eyebrows up and down menacingly.

Travis nudged his twin. "Uncle Nick has been re-incarnated as an angel." He peered at Krista. "And check out that good-looking cherub helping her."

Krista hid a shy smile behind one hand while a pretty blush highlighted her cheeks. Lyric gave Travis an approving glance. The Daltons were good for the female ego, and the child needed positive reinforcement.

After handing the youngster a glass of lemonade, Lyric took one for herself, then sat on the ground, joining the men in a semicircle under the tree.

The workers, including Jeremy and Tony, wore long-sleeved shirts, all open down the front, exposing muscular torsos with the rippling abs of exercise equipment advertisements. If any ad executives spotted them, they would be pestered until they signed contracts as models.

Or, she modified the thought, until the Dalton clan had had enough and would run the interlopers out of the county. They would be a formidable bunch to cross.

Beau, seated to her left, went to the station wagon and poured another glass of tea. Trevor offered everyone another serving of the peanut butter cookies, growling realistically if anyone took more than two and causing Krista to giggle.

When they were seated again, Trevor was beside Lyric while Beau had taken his place on the other side of Jeremy.

Lyric felt every nerve on her left side tingle with awareness as warmth spread over her. She suppressed an urge to lean into him, this strong, honorable man.

Nostalgia gripped her as she realized that one week from tomorrow she was supposed to get on the road and head back to Austin.

Home, she reminded herself firmly. Odd how distant Texas seemed at the moment. She gazed at the seven peaks on the western horizon as darkness rose in her. Trevor hadn't asked if she was leaving. He hadn't asked her to stay—

"Do you know the story of the seven devil monsters?" Beau asked Krista and Tony.

The kids shook their heads.

"They used to come over from Oregon and eat the children who lived here," he explained almost in a whisper and with great seriousness. He glanced over his shoulder as if to make sure no lurking monsters were listening.

He made a story of it, describing an Indian brave and the fair maiden he hoped to win in marriage, but first all the braves had to figure out a way to get rid of the monsters. They tried several tactics, but none worked.

"Coyote taunted the braves for their failure. Then

one day, Sun-Smiling, so named because her smile was as bright as the sun, made a mesh net out of long, tough meadow grass to gather roots for food. Coyote ran past her, laughing at his latest taunt to the braves. This made her angry. She chased him and tried to throw the net over him, but he was very fast and she couldn't catch him. However this gave Afraid-of-His-Arrows an idea.''

"Who?" Tony asked.

"Afraid-of-His-Arrows," Beau repeated.

Tony frowned, clearly not liking this name for their hero.

"He was such a fierce warrior and such a deadly shot with his bow and arrows that his enemies were frightened when they saw him riding into battle.''

Tony grinned. "They were afraid of his arrows.''

"Right.'' Beau ruffled the boy's hair and went on. "The brave and the maiden devised a plan. When Coyote went to his favorite place to nap the next afternoon after laughing at the latest attempt to capture him, Sun-Smiling followed and asked if he would like to use her finely woven net to keep the flies off his beautiful fur while he rested. Now, Coyote was rather vain. He thought this was a good idea and would help him have a good nap.''

"He's in big trouble,'' Tony declared.

"Right. The warrior pegged the net to the ground so Coyote couldn't escape, then they woke him. When he realized he was trapped, Coyote agreed to listen to the village elders and their problem. Upon hearing it, he called all the digging animals together and had them dig seven deep holes. He filled the holes with a magic liquid. The villagers made huge nets and put leaves on them to disguise the traps. When the monsters returned, they fell in the holes, which boiled and frothed around them so they couldn't get out. Coyote turned them into mountains, and there they stay to this day as punishment for their evil ways.''

''What happened to Sun-Smiling and Afraid-of-His-Arrows?'' Krista wanted to know.

''The villagers threw a big feast to thank the young couple and gave them seven beautiful horses as a wedding gift for saving the children, so all ended well.''

''However,'' Trevor added, ''all the people had to remember the names of the monsters or else Coyote said they would be able to return to life and be set free.''

''Does anyone know them?'' Jeremy asked, gazing at the distant peaks, his tone slightly mocking.

''Sure,'' Trevor answered. ''That's practically the first words out of a baby's mouth in these parts. But they're easy to remember. Three of them have *devil* in the name. He-Devil, She-Devil and The Devil's Tooth.''

Lyric saw Krista repeating the words to herself.

''Then there are the two mounts. Mount Baal and Mount Ogre,'' Trevor continued. ''The last two are The Goblin—think of Halloween—and The Tower of Babel, like in the Bible.''

Zack checked the time. "We'd better finish that field before Uncle Nick tells Coyote to turn us into skunks or something worse."

"Does Uncle Nick know Coyote?" Krista asked.

"Oh, sure," Beau said. "They're best friends."

"In that case, Krista and I had better go to the house and clean up our baking mess," Lyric said, rising. She gathered the two cookie bags, which were nearly empty. "Or maybe we should mix up some more cookie dough."

"More cookies," the four Daltons requested as one.

Laughing, she returned to the car while Krista stayed with her brother and cousin to help in the hay field. Lyric glanced back once as she drove off.

Trevor stood in the sun, his hair gleaming like ebony, his skin bronzed and glistening, while he watched her leave.

Perhaps she should ask Uncle Nick if Coyote would help her make a magic net to capture this handsome warrior. She smiled at the image this conjured in her mind.

Thursday dawned hot and bright. Lyric woke alone in her bed. Trevor had stayed at the stable with their prize stud, who had come down with a case of colic.

"Loco weed," Zack had decided after checking the pasture where the stallion had been grazing. "I'll fence off that section and spray out the weeds this weekend."

Uncle Nick had been disgusted with himself. "I should have checked on that. With all the other work, you boys have been too busy."

"We're finished with the hay for now," Trevor had reported. "I'll ride fences starting Monday and make repairs before it's time to bring the cattle down."

The talk around the dinner table was so familiar to Lyric, it brought a hitch to her heart. She and her parents and two brothers, along with the ranch fore-man, had often held the same type of discussions at mealtime.

After dinner, Trevor and his brothers had gone to the stable to check the horse. He'd volunteered to stay after Zack had purged the poor stud, which had looked as miserable as a horse could when she and the two youngsters had gone down to stroke his neck and sympathize.

Lyric rose, showered and dressed in a navy-blue linen dress with matching one-inch pumps. It was al-ready past seven, she noted, as she hurried down the hall of the west wing. They were to be at Seth's office around nine, then go to the branch courthouse at nine-thirty to sign in and be ready when the bailiff called their case.

She was nervous because they would have to ask the judge for a lot of leeway. Jeremy's uncle needed funds for a bigger house, which she was going to ask the foundation board to approve. Her father had as-sured her he had no problem with that and would talk to the other board members.

In the meantime, the two younger kids needed a temporary home. She was going to request that they be allowed to live with her until everything was resolved.

She thought of the situation between her and Trevor. In spite of the passion, she thought things weren't going to be settled very easily between them. He kept his heart under lock and key, his manner remote except when they made love.

"Good morning," her aunt said. "You're just in time."

The two older people were at the table. Breakfast was ready and in platters. From down the other hall, she heard the voice of the three runaways. They entered the dining room together. They were all dressed in creased pants and neatly pressed shirts. Their faces glowed with scrubbing. Their fingernails were clean and trimmed.

Uncle Nick and Aunt Fay had helped her supervise their preparations last night so they would be ready for court today. She let out a shaky breath, feeling as if the day would decide her fate, along with theirs, for all time.

"Eat up," Uncle Nick encouraged. "It may be a long haul until lunch."

"Where's Trevor?" she asked. "Isn't he going?"

His uncle shrugged. "The stallion isn't doing too well. He might have to stay here."

Lyric's spirits sank to her toes, but she kept the smile plastered on her face while she nodded, then quickly ate. By the time they left for town, the butterflies in her tummy had doubled.

The receptionist ushered the anxious little group into Seth's conference room and closed the door. Five minutes later he came in, approved their appearance and assured them they would do fine. "Answer only what's asked," he told them. "Tell the truth. Be polite."

Six heads bobbed in agreement.

"Don't get angry under any circumstance." He peered at his uncle.

Uncle Nick scowled, but nodded again.

Seth continued, "If a point needs clarifying, I'll ask more questions. Don't overexplain. The judge isn't stupid."

Lyric found herself staring at the door or straining to recognize a voice whenever she heard a faint sound from outside the room. She realized she was waiting for Trevor. She'd counted on his presence to bolster her courage.

"Speaking of the judge," Seth added, "the regular juvenile judge had a heart attack last night. Beau treated him and sent him to the cardiac surgeon in Boise. We'll see Judge Harrison this morning. He runs a strict court. Don't speak without getting his permission. Everyone clear?" he asked, ending his review.

There was murmured agreement. However, the two youngest ones looked rather frightened, and Jeremy already had a bit of truculence in the set of his mouth. They didn't expect the law to be fair to them.

The odd sadness descended on Lyric again. She inhaled deeply and rose when it was time to go, a fatalistic calm coming over her.

At the small branch courthouse, the group waited in an antechamber until the bailiff motioned for them to follow her. Although Lyric had been to court in several other cases, representing the foundation's concerns at the hearings, she found herself nervous about this one.

After waiting in another room for ten minutes, they were at last allowed into the judge's presence.

Juvenile hearings were often less formal than other courts, and that was true of this one. There were two long tables with several chairs, both facing a shorter table where the judge would sit.

To Lyric's shock, the social worker from Boise was seated at the opposing table. Mrs. Greyling didn't look up as the Dalton group filed in. She was busy with her notes and folders. Her manner was grim.

Seth, Tony and Krista sat at the table, while Jeremy, Lyric, Aunt Fay and Uncle Nick took chairs behind them. No one occupied the small gallery of chairs beyond that.

"All rise," the bailiff called out. "His Honor, Judge Ronald P. Harrison."

The judge entered and took his chair. "Be seated," he said. He spoke to Seth. "Are you ready, counselor?"

"Yes."

"And you, uh, Ms. Greyling?"

"Yes, Your Honor."

"Thank you for attending on short notice," the judge said to the woman, who gave a tight smile.

Before they could proceed further, the door opened and several people came in. Trevor, Travis, Zack and Beau, accompanied by the Dalton wives, murmured apologies to the judge and took seats. Trevor chose the empty chair next to Lyric. She shot him a quick, grateful smile.

"If we may proceed," the judge said rather brusquely. "This hearing concerns Antonio and Krista Aquilon, brother and sister. Are they present?"

"They are, Your Honor," Seth answered.

"The State's charges?" the judge asked.

Ms. Greyling explained that the children had been removed without permission from their appointed foster home by Jeremy Aquilon and that they had been missing for more than a year.

Krista turned to Seth anxiously. He smiled and shook his head slightly. She knotted her hands together and stared at the judge.

Judge Harrison studied the papers on his desk. "Jeremy Aquilon is eighteen. Are charges pending against him?"

"No," the woman said. "The district attorney decided the case wasn't strong enough since...since the children went to him."

"They ran away?" the judge asked sharply. He frowned at the woman, then perused the two children.

Lyric felt the dawn of hope.

"The man beat Krista," Tony said fiercely. "She dropped a plate—"

Seth put his hand on Tony's arm, quieting him. "Permission to speak, Your Honor?" he asked.

"Yes, go ahead. I want to get to the bottom of this."

"After his sister was severely whipped with a belt, Antonio left the house that night and went to his cousin. He asked Jeremy to take them someplace safe. Jeremy was himself a juvenile at the time. He lived with his uncle, Jefferson Aquilon, who also had taken in the other two, although there was no blood relationship between them."

"I thought their last name was the same."

Mrs. Greyling asked to speak and was given permission. She explained the confusing familial relationships.

Lyric was astonished to learn that Anthony and Krista had taken the Aquilon name after their mother married Jeremy's uncle, but the children weren't his.

After his father's death, Jeremy, having no one else, had also been taken in by the family. His aunt, who was related only by marriage, had kept the boy even after her husband died and she had hardships of her own in supporting three children. Meanwhile, Jeremy's uncle, Jefferson Aquilon, was in the Gulf War, then the hospital recovering from his wounds. When

Anthony and Krista's mother died during the accidental shooting, Jeff, just starting his business, had welcomed all of the orphans into his home. Until social services had taken the younger ones away.

Glancing to the side, she met Trevor's gaze, which acknowledged they'd both misunderstood the kinship bonds within the little band of orphans. They'd put two and two together, but it shouldn't have come up four. That was an assumption on their part.

The judge asked questions until he was clear on all points. "What do you recommend for the minors?"

"Family Services requests they be returned to custody for proper evaluation and placement in a proper home."

"No!" Tony and Jeremy said together.

The judge frowned at them. So did Seth. "There are other solutions, Your Honor," he said.

"I have an *amicus* brief from the Pedernales Foundation. Their representative has requested custody. Is Lyric Gibson present?"

"I am, Your Honor," Lyric spoke up.

"Your credentials indicate you're a sociologist—"

"She's the secretary for the foundation," Ms. Greyling interrupted.

"My title is executive director. I investigate all requests for grants. My opinion usually carries with the foundation directors, of whom my father is one."

"What does the foundation propose to do?" Judge Harrison asked.

"We will finance an addition to the home Jeremy's

uncle provided for the orphans. Family Services requires that each child have a bedroom. We have investigated the man and find him suitable in temperament and well able to provide a good home for Tony and Krista.''

''Did someone help you?''

Trevor spoke up. ''I did, Your Honor.''

''State your name.''

''Trevor Dalton.''

The judge's eyebrows lowered. ''Ah, yes,'' the judge said, ''the Daltons. I have a letter from Nicholas Dalton, also requesting custody of the children. I understand they are living at your home now?'' he asked the family patriarch.

''They are,'' Uncle Nick said.

Seth cut in smoothly. ''My uncle is willing to take the children until such time as Jefferson Aquilon is approved as a foster parent, or until they have reached their majority.''

''Your Honor,'' Ms. Greyling protested. ''Mr. Dalton is seventy-one years old. He's had at least one heart attack, and he's single.''

Uncle Nick cleared his throat. ''Miss Fay Gibson has done me the honor of accepting my proposal of marriage. We plan to marry before the end of the month.''

Fourteen faces reflected shock. Well, fifteen if one counted the social worker.

Even Seth forgot his lawyerly manners as the family members exclaimed and congratulated the smiling couple.

Lyric didn't move. She couldn't. A great abyss had just opened under her feet. Aunt Fay and Uncle Nick?

"Order," the bailiff called sternly, but there was a smile on her face. The judge glanced briefly to heaven as if seeking patience, then frowned at the notes in front of him.

"She's as old as he is," Ms. Greyling said, earning a dark frown from Uncle Nick and murmured growls from his nephews and the wives.

The judge surveyed them all. Instant quiet fell over the room. His eyes settled on the older man. "While you may live to be a hundred and twenty, the court would be remiss in placing two young, active children in an environment that could change rapidly with someone your age."

"There is Miss Gibson's solution," Seth suggested.

"What are your circumstances?" the judge asked her.

"I will provide a home for Tony and Krista, either in Lost Valley or in Boise, as the court sees fit. I'll also invite Jeremy to live there until he finishes high school and decides on his future. At another date, if it pleases the court, custody may be returned to Jefferson Aquilon."

"Ms. Greyling?"

"Your Honor, Miss Gibson not only isn't a resident of the state, she has no experience with children. At twenty-four, she is only six years older than Jeremy, much too young to provide the discipline needed in this case. And she is single.''

Lyric knew these were the objections that would be raised. ''I have worked with such cases in the past,'' she said. ''Seth Dalton has agreed to act as our advisor.''

Her argument was feeble at best. Hearing a murmur in the seats behind her, she waited for one of the Dalton couples who were already married to volunteer as foster parents in the interim.

No one spoke.

Seth addressed the judge. ''With the court's indulgence, Trevor Dalton has something to say on the situation.''

The judge nodded wearily, obviously resigned to everyone getting in on the act.

''Ms. Greyling apparently has forgotten that Lyric and I are engaged. We explained that when we went to her office to work out a solution for the kids. The Seven Devils Ranch was approved by the local Social Services office over twenty years ago. My uncle raised six orphans there. Lyric and I will make the ranch our home. We have more than enough bedrooms for Jeremy and his cousins to each have a room. With five adults in the house, there should be no concern regarding supervision.''

''Five?'' the judge asked.

''Jeremy is of age. He's done a darned good job of

caring for Tony and Krista this past year. I've found all three to be responsible and caring—''

"I get the message," the judge said. "And what are your wishes in this matter?" he asked the two minors.

"I want to stay at the ranch," Tony said. "If we can't go to Uncle Jeff."

"Me, too," Krista said eagerly. "I want to stay with Lyric and Trevor and Uncle Nick and Aunt Fay and the other orphans."

The judge jumped on that. "What other orphans?"

"The foals and calves. And the lambs. We have chickens, too," she added.

A ripple of laughter went through the gallery. The judge even smiled a fraction. He looked over the papers in the folder and the notes he'd jotted on a legal pad during the proceedings. Then he glanced at Ms. Greyling.

Lyric's heart sank. Not even the Daltons could sway this man.

"At present I am leaving Antonio and Krista in the care of—" he peered at the notes "—Lyric Gibson and Trevor Dalton. I'll expect a copy of the marriage license when we meet again next month," he added with a stern look. "Schedule it," he told the bailiff.

Lyric whirled on her chair to stare at Trevor. He returned the gaze, then smiled slightly, with something like irony...or resignation...in his expression.

"Looks like we'd better make plans for a double

wedding," he said, shifting his gaze to the older couple. "If you meant what you said."

His uncle nodded and took Aunt Fay's hand. "You heard the judge—we might not have much time. We intend to marry before the month is out."

"That's only one week from today," Lyric reminded them.

"You got a problem with that?" Trevor asked softly.

She hesitated, then shook her head.

"Let's get out of here," Seth murmured, "before his honor changes his mind." His dark eyes flicked to the older couple, then to Lyric and Trevor. "Or someone else does."

Chapter Twelve

Lyric left the courthouse in a daze. "Weddings don't come about like this," she murmured to Amelia.

Seth's wife patted her shoulder. "With this family one never knows," she said, laughter and sympathy in her tone. "Lunch at the B and B," she called out to the rest.

Trevor was standing behind the two women. He stepped up beside Lyric when Amelia headed toward her car. Lyric rushed to the ranch station wagon and slid in the middle seat with Tony and Krista.

"You can ride with me," Trevor said to Jeremy, his gaze on Lyric, his expression letting her know this was only a short reprieve.

Lyric knew they needed to talk, but she didn't feel

up to it at the moment. Maybe next year, or next century.

The hour hand was straight up when everyone tumbled out of their various vehicles in front of the Victorian B and B. The clan gathered around the ranch wagon and congratulated the older couple with laughter and bear hugs.

"I think congratulations are in order for Lyric and Trevor, too," Seth said. He shook his cousin's hand and gave Lyric a kiss on the cheek. "I hope you two are as happy as Amelia and I are."

"Thanks," Trevor said, his manner easy.

When he dropped an arm around her shoulders, Lyric nearly jumped out of her skin. His nearness seared along her side, and for the briefest second she wished they were alone and that he would sweep her into his arms and refuse to listen to any arguments on her part about why this was insane and impetuous and…and…

"Let's go inside," Seth suggested, holding the door and ushering everyone into the house. "I think a family discussion is called for, and a lot of planning."

Two round tables were already set in the great room. Soon food was placed on the sideboard, and everyone helped themselves to lunch. When Lyric was seated, Krista on her right, the chair to her left stayed conspicuously empty.

Two couples staying in the B and B returned from

a hike. They glanced around and immediately headed for the sideboard and the delicious food.

Amelia expertly prevented them from joining in by explaining it was a family celebration and inviting the foursome to fill their plates and take them to the outside patio. The guests did so while their hostess rolled her eyes at the family grouping.

Seth and Trevor came out of the kitchen, prepared plates and took the last two chairs, Seth between Amelia and Uncle Nick, Trevor between Lyric and Honey.

The conversation around the two tables covered the hearing in detail. Everyone agreed the sour-faced social worker was a pain, but the judge, scary at first, had turned out to be an okay guy.

"When are the weddings?" Zack asked, leaning past his wife to gaze at his brother and Lyric, then looking at the older couple. "Next weekend?"

Uncle Nick looked at his fiancée. She spread her hands in a hopeless fashion, as if surrendering to fate. The two elders smiled at each other while a swirl of love and envy and other emotions lodged in Lyric's throat.

Uncle Nick grinned. "The sooner, the better."

"At our age, we can't afford to waste any time," her aunt said. "According to Ms. Greyling, we might keel over at any moment."

That cracked everyone up. Krista put both hands over her mouth but couldn't suppress her delighted giggles.

Giving up on sorting through her mixed feelings, Lyric laughed, too. She decided if this was a hallucination, she may as well enjoy it.

Trevor murmured for her hearing alone, "I think that's the first time I've heard you laugh, really laugh, in almost a year."

Her laughter died as she stared into his ocean-deep eyes. If only he could see into her heart, then he would know how many times she had relived the joy of those three weeks in his company...and in his arms.

She looked at her plate, afraid her eyes would reveal the longing, the unbearable need to throw herself on him and demand that he trust her again. And that he love her.

But his faith in her integrity had been destroyed by her deception. Her fault. If only she'd explained the first time he'd kissed her, if only she'd had the courage to listen to her heart and trust its urging.

She'd been a coward. Now things were growing more complicated between them. Nicholas Dalton had raised his nephews with the concept of personal honor stamped on their consciences. They were decent, caring men. Trevor had stepped in when she'd needed help with the social worker and today with the judge.

His eyes had been grim, as if he'd faced a firing squad when he'd spoken in court. She couldn't bear the knowledge that he offered marriage out of duty when she ached for so much more. The tears fell but only in her heart where no one could see.

"A toast," Seth said, standing and heading for the kitchen. He returned with chilled bottles of champagne.

The Dalton wives brought out tall, stemmed flutes. Seth filled them to the top, except for the youngsters' glasses. For them, he poured two sips each.

When all was ready, he raised his glass. "To Uncle Nick and Aunt Fay. May your future be filled with joy for the full 120 years we are allotted on this Earth."

Everyone stood and cheered and drank to that.

Seth turned to the other couple. His smile seemed to become gentle as he gazed at them. "To Trevor and Lyric. May a bounty of blessings accompany you into marriage, and all the desires of your heart be fulfilled."

Lyric held the glass with both hands as tremors danced lightly over her body. Trevor moved close and settled a warm hand on the small of her back, steadying her while the others lifted their glasses and toasted the couple.

Tony inhaled as he sipped, got bubbles in his nose and sneezed explosively, spraying champagne across the table.

"Ah, a shower of blessings already," Uncle Nick said, patting his face with a napkin.

With laughter and good humor, they lifted their glasses once more, then resumed their seats while pie and coffee were served.

"We can have the reception here after the ceremony at church,'' Amelia volunteered as the planning for the weddings proceeded in earnest. ''The B and B guests love things like that. They always want to help.''

''What about you two?'' Travis asked. ''Does a week from Saturday work for you?''

''It's up to the lady,'' Trevor said gallantly, his smile only slightly mocking.

When all eyes turned to her, Lyric managed a calm—she hoped—manner. ''Well, my parents and my brothers will expect to attend. I don't know if they can take off on such short notice.''

''We'll check with them and let everyone know this weekend,'' Trevor inserted smoothly, covering her hesitation.

Was there going to be a marriage between them? She glanced at Trevor, realizing she wanted more than a duty marriage from him. She wanted intensity, joy, bliss—

''Of course they can,'' Aunt Fay said.

Lyric cast her aunt a questioning look, but the older woman was smiling at Uncle Nick as if he'd just hung the moon for her. Trevor eyed her in an aloof, amused manner that made her nervous.

He expected her to back off, she realized. She lifted her chin. Remember the Alamo and all that, she reminded her flagging courage.

''You ranchers can lounge around all day, but the rest of us have to work,'' Seth said, interrupting her fevered thoughts when the grandfather clock struck one.

His remark brought protests and threats from his cousins, which he totally ignored as he gave his wife a kiss, wished the engaged couples good luck, then headed back to his office.

Beau and Shelby also left for their afternoon medical appointments. Honey returned to the carriage house and her scheduled dance classes. Zack invited the three orphans to join him in working with the cutting ponies that afternoon since he had the rest of the day off from his deputy duties. Travis and Alison went home to relieve Jane Anne who was sitting with Logan. The senior couple declared they needed a nap after all the excitement and also left.

"Ready?" Trevor asked, standing by the door and waiting for her.

Lyric nodded. She thanked Amelia for lunch and was surprised when the other woman gave her a hug and whispered, "Dalton men make wonderful husbands. You won't be sorry."

Lyric gave her a troubled smile, knowing life rarely ended in a fairy tale.

Instead of driving directly to the ranch, Trevor stopped at the lodge owned by the Daltons. He eyed her shoes. "Can you walk in those?"

"Yes."

"Let's walk along the shore path."

He crooked his arm for her. Slipping her hand into

the warm angle, feeling the hard structure of his ribs against her wrist, she sighed, knowing they had to have this talk, but wishing they could merely stroll and admire the view.

"That bad, huh?" he asked, an unreadable smile curving his lips slightly as he guided her along the smooth, mulched trail beside the reservoir lake.

She shook her head. "I suppose things could be worse," she murmured lightly. "I wish they were simple."

He narrowed his gorgeous eyes and stared into the distance. The amusement was gone when he turned to her again. "Do you want to call it off?"

"The marriage?"

"Yes. I don't think the court is going to track what we do in the near future. If the foundation works fast, the kids can live with the uncle in Boise, then all will be resolved."

Lyric removed her hand from his arm. She stopped in the shade of a fir and pretended to admire the ducks bobbing for food. "I don't trust the social worker. I've never met one like her before. She's overworked as they all are, but she has an attitude. Why would she come all the way up here?"

"She's vindictive." He gave her a wry smile. "There, that's a simple diagnosis."

Taking her hand, he guided her to a bench under the tree, brushing it off with his handkerchief before letting her sit. While there were a few sailing prams on the lake, no one was using the path or fishing in their vicinity.

"What's it to be, Lyric?" Trevor asked. "Marriage? Or do you leave for Texas at the end of next week?"

He waited for the answer. Funny, but he didn't think his reaction would vary much no matter what she said.

An ache settled in him, more than one—in the groin, the throat and in the middle. The one in the groin was simple. He couldn't be around her and not want her. The one in his throat was caused by the knot of confusion she induced in him. The one in the middle was the one he worried about. It involved his heart.

Lyric was kindhearted, as her aunt had explained. She wanted to help the orphans. Would she marry him for that reason alone?

He wondered if a successful marriage could be built on a combination of passion and compassion. She murmured sweet endearments when they made love, but he didn't trust words spoken when the blood was running hot between them. That had been there from the first.

"Trevor, would you kiss me?"

His heart leaped like a stag's upon realizing the hounds were after it. He took in the rich highlights of the dappled sunlight in her hair, the velvet softness of her golden-brown eyes, looking at him so earnestly.

"Anything to please a lady," he said, angry with her at the unfathomable request, angry with himself for wanting her no matter what her reasons were for coming to him.

Darkness flicked through her eyes and was gone. She reached up and brushed the hair that always fell across his forehead with the gentlest of touches. Then she lifted her mouth to his.

He took the kiss deep, running his tongue along her lips until she opened to him, then plunging inside so he could plunder the honey of her mouth.

There was no one close by. He took advantage of that fact by sliding one arm around her shoulders and using his free hand to explore the curve of her torso, then letting his hand rest flat against her ribs. With his thumb, he stroked the underside of her breast.

Her response was instantaneous—a lifting of her chest, a quick intake of breath. The pain in his groin increased, but so did the one in his middle. None of that mattered, not as long as he held her and drank his fill of her.

"A public bench isn't a good place for this," he murmured, letting them come up for breath.

A faint smile touched her lips.

He stroked across the rosy surfaces which were warm from their kiss. "Did you find out what you wanted to know?"

Unexpectedly she laid her head against his chest and listened to the pounding of his heart. He could hear it, too, beating hard and regular like a drum.

Lyric pressed her face against his throat, the hot, thick urgency of despair filling her. She sensed that careful veil he kept between them, the withholding of the one thing she wanted most.

"I think..." She swallowed and took a deep breath. "I can't go back to Austin until the children are settled, but I think we should wait before going through with a marriage we may come to regret."

The muscles under her cheek flexed once, then slowly relaxed. She felt him exhale a long, careful breath. Lifting her head, she studied his face.

"But we continue the farce of an engagement?"

"For now," she said. "Is that all right?"

His face could have been a statue, it was so still. Then he smiled, a reckless, the-devil-take-the-hindmost kind of smile. "Who am I to complain? I'm getting the benefits."

He bent to her mouth once more and kissed her until she was weak with desire, until her blood raged, until her body demanded release from the overpowering hunger.

"Want you," she whispered as her world contracted to this one instant in his arms. "Now, Trevor. Now."

"I know a place," he said in a low, husky voice. He stood and held out a hand. "Come with me."

She didn't hesitate. Laying her hand in his, she ran along the path, back to the pickup. Inside, her heart pounding, she knew she would follow him to the end of the world and right over the edge.

* * *

Trevor stopped on the gravel road. Above them, through the trees, they could go to The Devil's Dining Room. Below, by following the faint trail through the pines, they would come to the cabin kept stocked for emergencies. By taking a logging road, he'd bypassed the ranch house. No one in miles knew of their presence.

He helped her out and led the way downward. The trail ended in a broad meadow where cattle grazed all summer. "In the fall, we round them up and drive them to winter quarters near the house," he said, seeing her eyes sweep over the herd. "It's too far up here. The cabin will be snowed in for four, five months."

At the rough wooden door, he removed the peg that held the latch before turning the knob and thrusting the door open. Even though the temperature in the sun was in the high seventies, chilly air rushed from the one-room cabin to envelope them. Lyric hugged her arms across her body.

"This was probably a stupid idea," he began.

"No," she said. "We couldn't be alone at the ranch house." Her gaze deepened, going dark as the centers enlarged when she stepped inside the line shack. "And I want to be alone with you."

All the aches shifted about and merged into one. Trevor opened the stubborn windows so the sun could heat the cabin. Going to a storage chest, he removed a couple of blankets and laid them over the two-inch foam pad that formed a mattress on one of the room's two cots.

He felt awkward, driven by needs he couldn't suppress, excited, but knowing this wasn't enough, that it would never be enough. With her, he wanted more than a lover's pleasure.

Finished, he faced her. She turned her back and held her hair to the side. Trembling slightly, he slid the zipper down her spine, then carefully peeled the dress from her body. It took only a couple of minutes to remove the rest. She helped him with his buttons.

When he laid the last of his clothing over the back of a chair, she sat on the bed, her back to the wall and watched, her eyes searing his skin with the passion she didn't try to hide.

Knowing he wouldn't be able to stop later, he removed a condom from a box he'd stored there previously, just before he locked his twin in the cabin, then abducted Alison, taken her there and left the two alone to work through their problems.

The ploy hadn't worked for them, he recalled. So much for playing cupid.

His mind went to more immediate things as he rolled a condom over the erection that had been paining him since the kiss at the lake. Lyric held up her arms when he turned to the bed. Her nipples were beaded, ready for him.

For a second he savored the sight of her bare body, liking the way the sunlight slanted through the window and fell over her shoulder, highlighting one breast as if spotting it for him.

He didn't need any more of an invitation. Near the exploding point already, he went to the waiting arms and the sweet caresses of the woman who could blow his mind with just a glance, a sigh.

"Trevor," she whispered when he sat beside her and gathered her close.

Her hands moved restlessly over him. She circled his navel with one finger, then trailed her fingers lower. She explored him thoroughly. He did the same to her.

Pressing her against the blanket, he pushed up on an elbow so he could see her full length. "I've never made love to you in daylight. It's a pleasure a husband can explore, but one rarely allowed in a clandestine affair."

He took the full measure of her ardor, from lips that were soft and moist to the rosy flush over her breasts, from the pale skin of her stomach to the smoothness of perfect thighs and delicate ankles.

Soft brown eyes studied him while he looked his fill. Finally she said, "Even husbands and wives must be circumspect in their daily lives."

"If there are others in the house," he agreed.

"If there are children," she added.

He cupped her breast in his hand, then leaned down to suckle the tight bud. Here, she would nourish their children. If they were to marry.

Touching her belly, he imagined it firm and

rounded. Here, she would carry the fruit of their passion. If they were to marry.

He stroked the crescent of bone that formed the Venus mound. To him, her structure felt delicate and special in ways he couldn't name. Molding his hand to her shape, he caressed her intimately, finding the slick heat that made him light-headed, knowing the pleasure to come.

"I wanted to do this...last year...from the moment we met," he told her. "It had to happen. I wanted to give you time...to love you slowly and win your trust."

"Shh," she pleaded. "Don't talk about last year. Love me now. Now!"

"I'm going to," he promised. "But it's going to be slow. It's going to be torture and bliss and everything in between. And when we can't stand it another second, when we come apart at the same instant, we'll do it all over again."

Putting her arms around his neck, she pulled him to her until their lips were less than an inch apart. "Then do it," she challenged. "Make me explode. Then put me back together and do it again." She laughed. "But watch it. Because I'm going to do the same to you."

She did.

He'd never physically suffered, but he did so now. Gladly. He gritted his teeth and tried to think of ice storms while she used her hands and mouth on him. Desire boiled through his veins, thick and rushing like a river bursting its banks, making him gasp with the effort of hanging on.

Revenge was sweet, he found.

He brought her to the brink, sobbing his name over and over, then he made her wait until her blood cooled before he started again.

They fought exquisite duels with their tongues. He panted. She moaned. She bit at his lips, angry and hungry. He tantalized her with his mouth at her breasts and lower, going very, very slowly until he dipped into the honeyed treasure. He tasted her passion again and again, unable to pull back from the delicate feast that was her.

But he pushed her too far.

An anguished cry reached him through the roar of his own pulse pounding in his ears. He felt her body shift under his hands, a wrenching twist as if she would tear herself from his grasp and flee. Her hands clenched in his hair, then she went perfectly still.

His control shattered. Rising, he positioned himself over her. She helped guide him home. Locking her legs around him, she pulled him deep inside.

It wasn't enough. He thrust deeper until they were welded into one perfect whole, their bodies touching everywhere while he devoured her mouth with his.

When she finally released her breath and moved against him, he joined the rhythmic flow. The roar inside his head increased, a tornado whirling through him, knocking aside the barriers that guarded his heart.

He was caught in a vortex of hunger and rage, pain and longing, the disillusionment of his youthful fantasies and the fulfillment of his wildest dreams. He'd known it could be like this. He'd known months ago…the first time he'd kissed her…he'd known.

The abyss of release was before him, coming straight and true, unrelenting and unstoppable now.

He heard her cry out and felt the internal pressure of her climax. It gripped him, stripping the last ounce of self-preservation from his soul.

Then he, too, was swept over the edge, the overpowering sensation like a wind, sweeping through his senses until there was nothing but this and her…*her.*

"Lyric," he said. "Lyric, my love."

Chapter Thirteen

Nicholas Dalton was startled when the door to his room opened and five strapping men entered, closing the door behind them. All five were in the prime of health, all blue-eyed and fair, except for one, whose dark eyes were filled with as much wicked amusement as the other four.

Nick crossed his arms and gave them a stern glare.

"Uncle Nick," Seth, the oldest, began, "we're here for The Talk."

"What talk?" he asked suspiciously. When he'd gotten up that morning, he'd expected to find all his underwear tied in knots or something. So far, he'd found nothing amiss.

The group settled in a semicircle around him, Beau

and Zack sitting in the reading chairs, Trevor and Travis on the chest at the foot of the bed and Seth propping a hip on the desk near the door.

This left him standing with his back to the wall. Literally. He leaned against the wainscoting and waited for the outcome as a smile tugged at the corners of his mouth.

"You rascals say what you have to say," he told them in as grouchy a tone as he could muster. "I've got things to do. This is my wedding day, you know."

The five nodded, their expressions somber.

"Dalton men are honorable," Seth intoned like a high priest delivering a commandment from the gods. "They keep their word and honor their vows. They take responsibility for their actions. Today you will make the most serious and lasting pledge of your life."

Zack took up the litany on marriage. "A man must build his marital house large enough to hold all that the woman will bring to it—children, family, friends, all those she loves."

"A man has to remember that, while time and energy must be spread between many duties, love multiplies. It never divides," Beau continued.

"Women are emotional creatures. Don't expect to go to bed on a quarrel and find welcoming arms," Travis solemnly instructed his favorite relative. "A man controls his appetites and thinks of others."

Nick smiled at the familiar words. Not only had the boys heard his little homilies, they'd remembered them. He swept his gaze over each one, these orphans he'd taken in twenty-three years ago. The house had been crowded, but so had his heart. He'd never regretted it, never for a minute. They were fine young men, every one of them.

His throat tightened with emotion as he waited for Trevor, the last Dalton bachelor, to parrot back one of his many lectures over the years.

Trevor hesitated. He really had no advice to hand out, not on the relationship between men and women. But the Dalton orphans had sworn to each other that they were going to give back every piece of advice the patriarch had given them if the opportunity ever presented itself. There was no time like the present. He assumed a wise countenance.

"Passion is a powerful drive and can last a lifetime," he reminded his uncle, "but there are many hours to fill between dawn and dark. A husband and wife need to be friends as well as lovers. They should respect each other for the qualities that drew them together and remember to forgive the ones that drive them up the wall."

He got the words out without faltering. He laughed with his brothers and cousins and slapped their uncle on the shoulder and wished him happiness. Then, as one, they became quiet. Each gave and received a hug from the man who had raised and nurtured them.

"Trevor," he said, detaining him when he would have left with the others.

Trevor paused.

His uncle closed the door, then studied him with a thoughtful frown. "I'd hoped we would be celebrating this day together. I was sorry when you and Lyric decided you weren't ready to commit to marriage."

Trevor ignored the pain in his chest. "There are questions that need to be answered before we can think that far ahead," he admitted.

"You're sleeping together," the uncle said bluntly.

He shrugged, unable to deny it.

"That's a powerful bonding tool. For most women it means love and commitment."

"For some," Trevor corrected with a cynical smile. "For Lyric, I think a person has to be among the abused, misused and generally downtrodden in life." He paused, then added, "I won't be weak to win her love."

His uncle thought it over, then nodded slowly. "She'll expend both emotional and physical energy on those who need her help. Her mate will have to be confident enough of his own worth to handle that."

When the older man gazed at him as if asking if he was that man, Trevor remained silent.

"When life drains her," the patriarch continued softly, "he'll be the one she turns to in her need. The man will have to nourish her from his own cup of life. He'll replenish her spirit, and through that giving, his own."

"That's asking a lot," Trevor said.

"It is. Ask yourself one thing—is your love big enough to do that? If not, you must let her go."

Another shaft of pain stuck in his chest. Trevor put a hand over his heart to shield it. "What will the man get in return?"

"Her unquestioning loyalty, her great capacity for compassion, the exclusive pleasure of her body, the generosity of her spirit when he is the one who needs to draw on it. Whatever else demands her attention, he will always be first in her heart."

"Sounds good," he said with forced casualness, "but will it play in Peoria?"

Something like disappointment flashed in the older man's eyes, then he stepped back as if distancing himself from the problem. He patted Trevor's shoulder. "Get out of here, you thick-headed mule, and let me finish getting dressed. This is *my* wedding day and I'm going to make the most of it."

Smiling at his uncle's frisky manner, Trevor returned to the middle of the house. A tiny brunette with Dalton-blue eyes threw her arms around him and tried to squeeze him to death. He hugged his cousin.

"Well, you two finally made it," he said to Roni and her husband, Adam. He shook hands with the man when Roni finally released him. "Good to see you, Adam. Roni said you'd been out of town most of the month."

"Testifying in L.A.," the FBI agent explained.

"The police corruption case," his girl cousin added.

"Ah, yes," Trevor said, "I remember it well."

Adam's sister, Honey, had come to the ranch with

Zack under the pretense of perhaps being Uncle Nick's missing daughter. She'd needed a place of refuge as the bad cops were looking for her in order to get to Adam.

"Has Honey told you our news?" Zack stopped beside the three with a grin on his face.

"Are you expecting?" Roni demanded.

"Next spring."

Trevor started as his cousin squealed like a banshee and threw her arms around Zack, then did the same to Honey, who carried in a box of flowers for the wedding party.

"What?" Honey asked, also startled.

"We're pregnant, too!" Roni exclaimed.

Trevor gave Adam a high-five, then stepped out of the way while all the women kissed and hugged and cried a little the way females did about the most natural thing in the world. What did they expect when husbands and wives slept together every night?

Spotting Lyric standing at the opening to the hallway with a quiet smile on her beautiful face, his heart gave a hard lurch. Her father was giving away the bride. Lyric was to be the maid of honor.

She was wearing a pink lace dress with a lace jacket. Honey handed her a bouquet of pink and yellow roses made from the blossoms in the front yard. A matching posy of rosebuds was nestled behind one ear.

His family had been disappointed that they didn't get to plan a double wedding when he'd explained he and Lyric had decided they wanted a longer engagement.

"Hey, we didn't want to cut in on Uncle Nick's and Aunt Fay's big day," he'd said.

The couple had delivered their announcement last Saturday night when the whole clan had gathered at the ranch for dinner and a planning session.

"Time to go," Seth called out. "Where's the bridal couple? They can't be late for their own wedding."

Trevor thought the week had gone smoothly. It should. The Daltons had had plenty of experience with weddings this past year. His brothers and cousins —all married.

"Who's Aunt Fay riding with?" someone asked.

"Me." Uncle Nick entered the living room in his Sunday suit and a new tie and shirt. Honey rushed to pin a boutonniere on his lapel.

"No, no," Roni protested. "You're not even supposed to see the bride before the wedding."

"She can ride with me," Lyric said. "Since I brought her here, it's appropriate that I should deliver her to the church, too."

"Can I ride with you?" Krista begged.

"Of course."

"Jeremy and Tony are with me and Honey," Zack said.

Seth took charge. "It's settled, then. I'll drive Uncle Nick in. He won't need the ranch wagon since they'll be at the B and B overnight, then I'm driving them to the airport for the trip to Texas in the morning."

Trevor glanced at Lyric at the same moment she looked at him. Their eyes held for a long second, then they both turned elsewhere.

"Go, go," Roni ordered. "Take Uncle Nick. The bride comes last."

She herded them out the door like a small shepherd directing a noisy, stubborn flock.

Trevor waited with Lyric as silence fell over the room. "I'll follow you in just to make sure nothing happens to your car," he told her.

"Lyric? Isn't it time to go?" her aunt called out.

Trevor felt his heart swell as the older woman came into the room. She wore a simple white lace outfit very similar to her niece's. Lyric removed a bouquet of white roses ringed with pink and yellow roses, each tipped with a soft pink blush, from a box and handed it to the bride.

Aunt Fay took it with trembling fingers and inhaled the sweet fragrance. She smiled at her bridesmaid. "I'm nervous. I didn't think I would be, but I am."

"It isn't every day a girl gets married." Lyric smoothed the lace attached to a tiny bridal hat perched on her aunt's head, her touch so very gentle, her smile supportive.

Trevor swallowed against the hard place in his throat. "Let's hit the road. We have an appointment in—" he checked his watch "—exactly fifty minutes."

He tucked the two women into Lyric's car, then fell in behind it with the pickup. The trip was both fast and slow. At the church, he escorted the two women into the vestibule, then alerted the others that the bride was there. As he'd expected, the church was packed to the rafters.

Lyric's mother and brothers were the occupants of the bride's pew. The Daltons occupied an entire row on the other side of the aisle. Mr. Gibson quietly entered from a side door. "Ready?" he asked, looking into his aunt's eyes with a worried smile.

"I should be. I've been waiting for thirty years for this moment," she replied in her usual fashion.

Trevor realized his uncle had married her cousin thirty years ago that past June. He took a deep steadying breath.

To love someone that long. To think for years and years that there wasn't a chance of fulfilling that hope. An ache settled in his chest as he headed for his seat.

Love, he decided, wasn't all it was cracked up to be. In fact, it was a damned painful experience.

The ceremony at the church went off without a problem. Lyric thought it beautiful and solemn and spiritual. When the minister said, "I give you Mr. and Mrs. Nicholas Dalton," thus ending the ritual, she and the sheriff, who was the best man and Uncle Nick's oldest friend, followed the married couple down the aisle to the applause and cheers of the audience.

Her eyes met Trevor's as they passed. She looked

away as her heart wheeled and dipped like a hungry hawk. At this moment she could have been holding his arm. She could have walked down the aisle as his bride.

If she'd said that was what she wanted. If she'd been willing to accept him without complete trust between them.

After waiting for the photographer to snap about a thousand pictures, they went to the B and B, where a huge feast awaited them. Tables draped in pink and yellow linens spilled over from the great room to the patio outside.

She sat at the bridal table along with her father and two brothers. Her mother was there, too. Aunt Fay had called and insisted the other woman attend. The family had flown out together. They would return to Boise that night and fly back to Texas the next morning.

Lyric wondered if she should return to Austin, too, until the hearing before the juvenile judge next month. Her father had brought approval from the foundation's board to grant the housing request. The local chapter of Habitat for Humanity was planning a blitz build of a four-bedroom home for the Aquilon family, which would be finished before winter set in.

All was well.

A haunting melody wafted through the room, bringing a momentary hush. Uncle Nick stood and held out his hand to his bride. People moved aside, opening an area near the front door. The couple performed a flawless waltz.

To Lyric they seemed young and graceful, as if they were just starting down the road of life.

"Ready, sweetheart?"

She blinked, then looked at her father in question. "Oh," she said, realizing it was their turn.

While her father danced with Aunt Fay, Lyric danced with the groom. When the sheriff cut in on her dad, Amelia claimed the groom. Lyric peered around for her father, but he was already leading her mother forward.

Another pair of arms twirled her about. She looked up at Trevor with tears in her eyes. He offered his hankie.

"It's just that it's all so lovely," she explained.

He stuck the handkerchief in his pocket when she returned it after dabbing at her eyes. "Yeah, it is," he said, his eyes riveted on her.

The breath went right out of her body.

"Don't look at me like that," she managed to say.

He pulled her closer. "Tell me to stop wanting you," he growled low in her ear. "Tell my heart to stop beating."

"My turn," a male voice interrupted.

She was whisked away before she could respond to Trevor. From over her older brother's shoulder, she stared at Trevor as he cut in on one of the Daltons dancing with her aunt. His eyes were dark, mysterious, filled with thoughts she couldn't read. She thought the music would never end.

"I can see your thoughts are elsewhere," her brother murmured, following her gaze. "Seth said you two were, uh, sort of engaged. Are you?"

"No. Yes." She clamped her teeth into her lower lip to hold the words inside.

Her brother grimaced. "Sheesh. Can't women ever make up their minds?"

"Yes," she said softly. "We can."

He dipped his head and stared into her eyes. "What are you plotting?"

"A test of honor," she told him.

At last the cake was cut, toasts were given and the bridal pair went to their honeymoon suite. The festivities were over. After kissing her family, Lyric waved from the front porch until they were out of sight, heading for Boise and the flight that would take them back to Texas.

She spoke privately to Amelia in the kitchen as she helped clean up. "I don't think I'll need that room tonight after all."

"Are you going back to the ranch?" Amelia asked, a gleam coming into her eyes.

Lyric nodded.

"Good girl," her hostess whispered. "Trevor needs you. Don't let pride keep you apart."

Lyric slipped out of the quiet, charming Victorian into the soft purple shadows of twilight. The wind, cool with the coming night, caressed her, blowing down from the mountains as if ready to guide her to the far peaks.

Getting into her car, she drove slowly, thoughtfully, to the ranch, the road now as familiar to her as the one leading to her childhood home.

Only Trevor's pickup was parked at the wooden railing in front of the ranch house. She stopped next to it and climbed out, all her doubts returning in a rush.

Before she could cut and run, she forced herself across the lawn, onto the porch and into the house. Trevor came down the hall, dressed in working clothes. It was time for the evening chores. He stopped at the archway into the living room.

"What are you doing here?" he asked.

She could detect nothing but curiosity in his tone. "I've decided we should get married right away."

He blinked once, then his face changed subtly, as if a veil had been drawn over his features. His smile was brittle. "Women always get sentimental at weddings. You'll get over it."

She shook her head. "Your uncle said you were an honorable man. Are you?"

A frown knit a line between his beautiful eyes. "I try to be. What are you getting at?"

"The truth." She inhaled deeply, reaching for courage. "You called me 'your love' the other night. Am I?"

"Men say things in passion," he began, then stopped.

The planes of his face seemed to become harsher as he stared at her. He resented the question, she realized, but he couldn't deny the answer. He couldn't lie to her.

"I love you," she said softly. "I've come a long way to tell you that."

"Am I dying of something I don't know about?" he asked with an ironic edge. "Or have you decided you really do need a husband so you can help the orphans?"

Despair filled her. Again she'd waited too late to tell him how she felt. He thought she spoke out of need. It came to her that she did.

"I do need you," she said, taking a step toward him, then another. "I need you to complete my life, to stop the empty ache inside my heart, to fill my days with joy and my nights with passion. I need you, not for others, but for myself. I need your love…and your trust."

Trevor saw the desperation in her, felt it in himself. He recognized the moment as a pivotal one. He could accept her declaration as the truth and take the bliss thus offered. But that came with a price.

Trust.

In giving that, he would also have to accept the past, knowing that she'd chosen another over him.

Because of her own sense of loyalty and principles.

"'This above all, to thine own self be true,'" Uncle Nick had once read to the orphans gathered around him. "'And it must follow, as the night the day, thou canst not then be false to any man.'"

Lyric sighed quietly. She'd done all she could, but Trevor would never give her his trust as he once had. "I'm sorry," she whispered, feeling the fountain of tears welling up inside her. "I shouldn't have come."

"No," he said. "It's okay."

"I'm going home. To Austin," she continued, keeping her voice steady. "Jeff will soon have a home for the kids, so there's no need for me to stay. I can handle the details from Texas." She managed a laugh. "You won't have to come to my rescue with fake engagements…"

She turned and fumbled blindly for the door as her throat filled with the treacherous tears.

"I need you," Trevor said behind her.

Finding the doorknob, she stood there, afraid to go forward, afraid to look back. She shook her head.

"I do," he insisted. "I need someone to fill the empty places in my heart…and the lonely hours of the night." His voice dropped so low she could barely hear it. "You must know that I love you."

Hands on her shoulders turned her.

"Look at me," he ordered. "Look at me and tell me you can leave behind what we have and never regret it."

Seconds, minutes, eons passed.

"I can't," she said.

"Neither can I. I love you, Texas gal, too much to let you go."

The tears crowded into her eyes, spilled over. "I never thought I'd hear you call me that again."

His lips touched her eyelashes. He sipped the tears from them. "You'll hear it from now on," he promised. "I am an honorable man, and honor demands marriage. Agreed?"

She brushed the stubborn lock of hair from his forehead. "Yes."

The word hardly left her mouth when she was caught up in a rapturous kiss that left her trembling when they at last came up for air. "I think we had better call the newlyweds and tell them not to extend their honeymoon, as they're needed for another wedding," he murmured, leading her to the sofa and settling there with her in his lap.

"And next month we can tell that smirky Ms. Greyling we are truly married," Lyric said with great satisfaction.

A flash of emotion passed through his eyes, but his smile was tender as he gazed at her.

Lyric cupped his precious face between her hands. "Last year, when you left, it was as if a part of me, something that was basic and necessary, disappeared, too," she explained, the words coming painfully. "When I gave you up, when I thought I couldn't have your love because of what I owed to others, I gave up part of my own soul. I'll never do that to us again."

Trevor nodded, believing her. She would keep her word because that was the way she was. Loyal and caring and compassionate. She had a big heart, and he would have to share parts of her, but the most important part—that part of her that loved him exclusively—was his forever.

Perhaps they both had had to learn some lessons about life before they could come to each other openly and in total trust. He smiled and inhaled her special fragrance, filling his lungs, his heart, his soul with her.

Like the wildflowers covering the valley in springtime, love grows and multiplies and takes root in all who dare open their hearts to it.

Pulling her close, he opened his heart as wide as it would go. There was room, he discovered, for her, for the children she would give him and for those she brought into their lives. Plenty of room for all.

Just like Uncle Nick's.

* * * * *

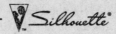

From

Silhouette®

SPECIAL EDITION™

Patricia Kay

presents her next installment of

The HATHAWAYS of

MORGAN CREEK

A dynasty in the baking...

HIS BEST FRIEND

(January 2005, SE #1660)

When wealthy Claudia Hathaway laid eyes on
John Renzo, she was blown away by his good
looks and sexy charm. He mistakenly gave her
the wrong contact information and so was gone
forever...or so she thought. The next thing she
knew, she was dating his cousin and caught
in a love triangle!

Available at your favorite retail outlet.

eHARLEQUIN.com

The Ultimate Destination for Women's Fiction

Visit eHarlequin.com's Bookstore today
for today's most popular books at great prices.

- An extensive selection of romance books by top authors!
- Choose our convenient "bill me" option. No credit card required.
- New releases, Themed Collections and hard-to-find backlist.
- A sneak peek at upcoming books.
- Check out book excerpts, book summaries and Reader Recommendations from other members and post your own too.
- Find out what everybody's reading in Bestsellers.
- Save BIG with everyday discounts and exclusive online offers!
- Our Category Legend will help you select reading that's exactly right for you!
- Visit our Bargain Outlet often for huge savings and special offers!
- Sweepstakes offers. Enter for your chance to win special prizes, autographed books and more.

**Your purchases are 100%
guaranteed—so shop online
at www.eHarlequin.com today!**

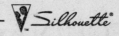